I0724358

Queer As Fiction

stories

Spineless Wonders

PO Box 220

Strawberry Hills

New South Wales, Australia, 2012

https://shortaustralianstories.com.au

First published by Spineless Wonders 2021

Editorial assistance by Prashant Prasad. Production assistance by Olivia Garcia and Madeleine Warburton.

Typeset in Adobe Garamond Pro

Printed and bound by Ingram Spark Australia
Queer As Fiction An anthology of short stories
1st ed.

ISBN 978-1-925052-68-8 (pbk)

A catalogue record for this book is available from the National Library of Australia

Queer As Fiction

stories

Edited by

Bronwyn Mehan & Ygraine Heloise

spineless wonders

www.shortaustralianstories.com.au

Content

Illustrations by Ygraine Heloise

Introduction

Quinn Eades

Dear Queers,

I'm writing this letter to you from the second week of a fifth stage four COVID lockdown. It's cold and the kids are remote schooling. I've learnt to write to the sounds of horse's hooves, machine guns and zombies. The kids call their friends to play online and discuss portals and maps and sniper positions and glitches. On the news everything is wrong and it's hard not to feel like it's the end of the world.

I've been thinking about living in the ruins after re-reading Donna Haraway's *Staying with the Trouble*. In 'Children of the Compost', a collaborative speculative fiction project, she describes a utopian movement founded on the understanding that when things fall apart we must learn to live on and in and under our broken grounds. "They asked and responded to the question of how to live in the ruins that were still inhabited, with ghosts and with the living too." I think that those of us on the margins, the ones who do not fit, have always lived in the ruins, and one of the ways we do this is to tell each other our stories – to remind each other of who we are.

Queer as Fiction is a collection that understands what it is to tell stories for us that are by us, and reading it gives me the feeling of coming to a kind of home. This home is full, is teeming with queer language and love, is a home where I recognise myself in the mirror, and where people remember my name. Each story holds its own, but as I read, they mingle, make a shining threaded net. They find each other in grief, loss, art, abandonment, work… In corners and on edges, in the silvery glimmer of day turning to night. And again and again, in and with the body.

As I read, I think about touch. On the news the other day I heard a psychologist say that humans need to be touched a minimum of seven times a day. I think of the feeling of being skin hungry, of not being touched, of not having touched enough. How furtive we have to be sometimes just to brush up against each other. As I read, I think about time. About this precious writing gathered here, these coming out and in and to each other stories, that make a queer archive of our bodies and loves in this particular present, in the ruins, at the end of one kind of world. By the time I have finished, I have come home to the page.

It's suddenly dark and the kids are asking for dinner – I've been holding them off with muesli bars and mandarins. I miss you. I miss being out with you when everyone else has gone to bed. I miss drag shows and kisses on the dance floor I miss touching and shouting and fucking I miss glitter on my pillow the next morning.

Stay safe beautiful ones.

With much love,
from unceded Wurundjeri land,
Quinn xxx

Who needs the dictionary anyway?

Phoebe Lupton

Heteronormativity

[heh-teh-roh-nor-mah-ti-vi-tee]

noun

apparently, everyone is straight.

*

Disney princesses are her heroes. Her goal in life is to be Belle from Beauty and the Beast. She doesn't realise that this story is, as Otis Milburn from Netflix show Sex Education would say, "classic imposter syndrome." All she sees in fairytales are their happy endings, the brave prince saving the helpless princess, and at least in Beauty and the Beast it's the princess saving the prince. She loves the long, flowing, colourful gowns. She aches to live in a magic castle, talk with birds and do nothing all day but sing.

She learns that the girls who are the main characters in Disney films are conventionally pretty, stylish and straight. There are no stories about a princess falling in love with a princess or a prince falling in love with a prince, and there certainly aren't any stories about people who are neither princes, nor princesses. She starts to believe that her life is one big fairytale. Everyone in her little world is a Disney character: her mum's the Fairy Godmother from *Cinderella*, her dad's King Triton from *The Little Mermaid*. As for herself, she's every single princess combined, a Super Princess, with all the fancy dresses and singing prowess in the lands.

The people she's met so far in her short life all seem to sit within the binaries that her favourite fairytales have introduced her to. At least, that's what she thinks. Years later, she'll discover that her auntie only likes women and her uncle only likes men, and as she grows older, she'll discover that even she herself doesn't completely fit the princess model.

But right now she's too young, too impressionable, too susceptible to the lies spread throughout the world about what love is and who can access it. She is blocked from reality, living solely in her dreams. When she imagines her future, she pictures a big house, a big garden, a husband, a son, a daughter and animals that can speak English. It's only when she gets a little bit older that this vision begins to melt away.

Fast forward to Year 3, and she meets a girl in her class who has two mums. The concept of 'two mums' doesn't compute at first. Until now, she's believed that all little boys and girls have a mummy and a daddy. She goes home and tells her mum what she's found out.

"Your friend's mums are gay people," her mum explains. "They are ladies who only fall in love with other ladies."

"Hmmm. Okay," she says, even though she still doesn't quite get it.

And then her mum tells her about her auntie and her uncle, and she starts to wrap her head around it. Every now and then she goes to play at her friend's house and sees this friend's two mums, who are just like her own mum and dad except that they're both ladies, whereas her parents are a lady and a man. What's the difference, anyway?

*

Bisexuality

[by-secs-yoo-al-it-ee]

noun

turns out, you can like both girls and guys.

*

At first, she learns of 'straight' and 'gay'. They start to make sense, but she doesn't know which one fits her yet. When she's twelve, she discovers the word 'bisexual'. She finds a YouTube clip of an *X Factor* performance in the United Kingdom, in which a man called Danyl sings 'And I'm Telling You' from *Dreamgirls*. One of the judges says:

"If we're to believe everything we read in the papers, maybe you didn't need to change the gender references."

At first, she doesn't understand what this woman is saying. Falling into the YouTube rabbit hole she's apt to fall into, she clicks on an interview with that judge, Dannii Minogue. In the video, Dannii explains that she'd made that 'gender references' comment because she'd heard that Danyl was bisexual.

It would be many years until she would think about that term in relation to herself. But even now, the image of herself as 'straight' is beginning to crumble. Singing in an all-girls choir, she becomes fascinated with another girl.

This girl is beautiful, with waist-length hair the colour of gold and a pearly-white smile that brightens the sky. She can't take her eyes off her. At this time, she thinks she wants to be like this girl. She herself has hair the colour of Nutella, and peach fuzz lines her lips. All her life, she's wanted to look like this girl with gold hair. But the feeling that all but consumes her when she looks at this girl is not jealousy. Her brown eyes do not change to green, her stomach does not turn over at the idea of this girl being more beautiful than her. She doesn't realise that the feeling in her bones is a crush.

As she grows older, she falls in love with guys, and with some girls, and probably with people who are neither. At seventeen, she has another crush that she doesn't realise is a crush. This time, it's on a teacher. She experiences a duality of urges: to be around her teacher, to not be around her teacher; to get closer to her teacher, to withdraw from her teacher; to love her teacher, to hate her teacher. This duality comes from disgust at herself. She doesn't understand why she's so drawn to this person, someone who holds authority over her and who is, you know, the same gender as her. It takes months and months of self-analysis – and YouTube binge watching – to name this experience for what it is: fancying an older woman.

Throughout her seventeenth and eighteenth years, 'bisexual' runs through her head like a hamster on a wheel. Heteronormativity obstructs her ability to identify with this word, but she eventually pulls herself away from its steel grasp. At nineteen, she claims 'bisexual' as her own for the first time.

*

Pansexuality
[pan-secs-you-al-it-ee]

noun

actually, you can like pretty much anyone.

As she enters her twenties and embarks on a journey of feminist self-discovery, she learns more about the word she's adopted. She likes 'bisexual'. It's simple, both in phonetics and etymology. She learns about other words, too: pansexual, asexual, aromantic, as well as trans, nonbinary, agender, genderqueer.

Fewer people than she thought fit into boxes. The gender binary works for her, but not necessarily for everyone else. She realises that labels aren't tattooed onto people's foreheads. They belong inside of them, in their hearts and minds and the very things that make them human.

Genital preferences don't gel with her brain. When she sees someone beautiful in the street, she sees their smiles, their spirits. She doesn't see what's in their pants. Masculinity and femininity and androgyny are irrelevant to her. She falls for men who wear makeup, women who wear suits, nonbinary folks who wear beanies and bucket hats. Love comes from personality, from something intuitive and magical and lively. Her crushes rarely discriminate.

A compulsive Googler, she craves to know more about labels. Reading up on bisexuality and pansexuality, she can't tell the difference. 'Bisexual' is more common, more widely understood, but 'pansexual' works just as well for her. She starts watching *Schitt's Creek* and notices David Rose's analogy to describe his own sexuality:

"I like the wine and not the label."

She understands David like she understands the sky is blue. As she progresses with the show, she witnesses David having a short-lived fuckbuddy relationship with his female friend Stevie, accidentally entering a thruple, and ultimately meeting the love of his life, Patrick. She buys an oversized t-shirt that reads, Into the wine, not the label.

But still, she can't pick a label. She tries on two different sets of clothes, and both of them fit. Yet, she bathes in the idea of two labels, of two parts of one identity that make up a whole person. So, she adopts a second child named 'Pansexual.'

*

Queer

[kw-ir]

adjective

maybe, it doesn't really matter.

*

All her life, she wanted to be part of something. She's lucky now. With the opportunity to enter a community that champions unconstrained love, for others and for oneself, she can squeeze herself under the umbrella of 'queer.'

She's always liked this word. Having come out at the tail end of the 2010's, a decade much more accepting than those which came before, she never had 'queer' thrown at her like golf balls in the playground. To her, 'queer' is non-normative, but okay anyway. To her, 'queer' is a team to which she belongs, someone who understands her and welcomes her like family.

'Queer' can also mean questioning, undecided, not quite sure. She's bisexual and pansexual, but she's also confused. It's rare for her to fall for someone these days. She can go months without feeling an ounce of wanting to get into someone's pants, or even wanting to hold someone's hand. Love isn't always satisfying. She knows of 'asexual' and 'aromantic', but they don't fit neatly inside of her soul like 'bisexual' and 'pansexual' do.

Sometimes, she only likes women. Sometimes, she doesn't like women but does like everyone else. Her heart is as fluid as water, changing and moving so fast, it's hard for her mind to keep up. And she's okay with this. Whilst before she squirmed at the unknown, now she sits with it like she does a pillow. With all the people she's met, all the strangeness in the world that humans have created, she's learnt that nothing can be predicted. Complexity can't be reduced. Humanity can't always be explained by the inanimate. Queerness can't be denied as an inevitable part of life.

She still likes labels. They help her name what otherwise can't be named, touch what otherwise can't be touched. But she can't pick one, or even two. She wants the power to change her mind, to change words and morph them into something that suits her better. Who needs a dictionary when you have self-discovery?

As an adult, far older and wiser than the little girl copying out drawings from Beauty and the Beast, she knows she's the dictator of her own life. She is powerful. She is bisexual, pansexual and queer. But she's also just...human.

My Strawberry Tea

Isabelle Quilty

I enjoy my tea, knowing this cup isn't mine, but hers. It's painted with dainty roses, lilacs, and daisies. That's what she calls the splashes of colour she's dashed onto the ceramic. Sunlight pours like warm honey onto my skin, from a window we can't open anymore. The paint and age of the house has locked it closed forever, so that I might watch the birds outside dance from branch to branch but can never catch a falling feather. Rain glances off the glass, mimicking the drip of the kitchen faucet. I wait for her to return; I've never been strong enough to squeeze the handle hard enough.

My place has always been the artist, and her, the pragmatist. My paint strokes drew on the strength of her muscles, the knowing deftness of her hands as she fixed the many quirks and broken pipes of our house. Her paint strokes disguised the old wood of the creaking porch, where I set my canvas down during the pale light of winter dawns.

Those winter nights brought fierce storms, and I was the one to hold her. She shivered and whimpered but refused to admit her fear of the thunder crashing outside our window, or the rain lashing the side of the house. More than thunder and rain weighed down on her, I could sense it, but I never asked. I reasoned that if I never asked, then the tension in her shoulders and shake in her hands would go away. For a while, it did, then it came back the next month, worse than ever after her mother called her.

How long had it been since her mother had called? Not long enough. As Autumn turned the backyard to hues of orange and auburn, she made a habit of fielding phone calls with a cigarette between her lips. The calls became more constant as her mother worsened. She never told me, but I knew. We would share a cigarette on the back porch, kicking wet, dead leaves off the porch, and the silence between us told me everything.

We repeated this, over and over until another year passed, the phone calls bleeding deep into the night. I had no one to hold and protect from thunderstorms anymore, or anyone to fix the leaking taps.

But one afternoon, as rain splattered on our shoes as we shared a cigarette, she finally broke the silence. She asked me a simple question, that should've had a simple answer. Should she be the one to look after her mother?

I took a sip from the teacup and shook my head. I replied to her with a simple two-letter word and shrugged.

We never talked about it again. To me, it meant all was well. I should've known better. I should've known that those phone calls didn't stop, she just stopped picking up. She stopped coming to me when it thundered, instead, she hugged a pillow and cooed softly until the weather passed. The taps were never fixed, and they continued to fall apart one little bit at a time.

I noticed but chose not to acknowledge it. If I didn't ask where the rest of our cups and plates got to, I could imagine she wasn't smashing them out at the old quarry. If I didn't ask about the rubbish bags of beer cans stuffed behind the shed, I could pretend I didn't smell it on her breath.

She'd begun to smell like her mother. Her mother, who when she tried to introduce me, pulled a fistful of hair from my head and screeched that I had been the one to make her daughter like women. She insisted her daughter was a good girl, innocent and faithful, and I had seduced away from the life of a good honest woman. After that introduction, we moved a long, long way away. So far away she could only reach us through the phone.

It was summer again when the calls finally stopped. I'd been out the back trying to paint again, and steady my shaking hands, the cicadas roaring and falling silent when she stepped out and kicked my paints and tub of water over. The water and paints mixed over the ugly veneer of the rotting porch, forming bright hues of orange and red.

Hands stuffed in her pockets, she gave the same look her mother had, the one that called me a monster, and said nothing.

The next day, she was gone. She took nothing with her, except for her car and her pillow.

My pragmatist went, I remember in the brush strokes, and strawberry tea I drink from the cup she left. The strokes of my paintbrush don't remember her strength or the final look she gave me, but the part me she showed me when the storms washed over our home.

As the rain runs down the windowpanes, the droplets leaking through the glass, I drink my tea and examine what may well be the last thing I ever paint.

On the thin canvas, there she was. In our kitchen, she stood making a cup of tea with that wide, dimply smile of hers. In the window outside, it was a warm summer's day.

Cross-dressing in Kathmandu

Brooke Maddison

Rani applied the thick kohl eyeliner with precision as she squinted at the grimy mirror above the sink. She patted down her colourful sari before reaching into her makeup bag and taking out a packet of elaborate bindis. She offered us one each, cocking her head playfully to the side.

'Jaanu?' Let's go?

'Jaanu.' We wobbled our heads from side to side. Let's go.

We swayed into the dark alleyway, a little unsteady on our high heels. Rani took the lead, guiding us through the twists and turns of the dimly lit lanes. The night bore down on us, holding the promise of the unknown and the forbidden. All that is obscured during the brightness of day is free to play in the shadows of night.

With a final turn, we emerged from the alley and were thrust onto a street thronging with people and motorbikes. Neon lights blinked down on Kathmandu's inhabitants as they hurriedly went about their lives, oblivious to the secrets hidden underneath Rani's clothing. Rani stepped onto the road, in front of the incoming traffic, and with the flick of her wrist, hailed us a cab.

My friend and I concertinaed our saris into the backseat as Rani reeled off the name and location of the nightclub to the driver. The sounds of the street fell away as we were momentarily cocooned from the outside world yet again. My Nepali was rudimentary, so the rapid-fire conversation between Rani and the driver washed over me as I watched the city rushing past my window. I was clueless to the negotiations and flirtations going on in the front of the taxi. But out of the corner of my eye I saw Rani's hand reach over and rest suggestively in the driver's lap.

We turned off the main road and the taxi bumped down a dimly lit dirt road. Eventually we came to a stop next to a rundown building. I could make out the faint sounds of music coming from within the building—a mixture of Nepali pop and Bollywood hits. We were just beyond the centre of the city, but it seemed so far removed from the gaudy yet comforting tourist district of Thamel that my friend and I had been exploring for the last two months.

Rani turned to us and indicated that we should get out of the taxi and wait for her. The tiny Maruti taxi lingered for a moment then lurched forward and turned around a dark corner. We stood in our heels and saris, with our hair and makeup done. It was the first time that we had been dressed up like this after months of travelling through India and Nepal. It felt strange, but exciting.

There was no question in our minds as to what was going in the front seat of that taxi.

Transgender, gay, cross-dressing, drag—these words had no place within the Nepali language. I had often been told by Nepali friends that there was no homosexuality within Nepal. Because without the language to define an identity, how could it exist? Within the language, the spectrum of queerness simply didn't exist. There were no words for lesbians, bisexuals, trans or non-binary folk. No words for intersex or asexual people. And without the words, I was told that these people didn't exist within the country.

At the time, the LGBTQIA+ community in Nepal was limited to the 'MSM' scene, men who have sex with other men. Within this terminology, men were either seen as being ta or meti—which roughly translates as masculine and feminine in English. Ta's are 'straight' and hyper masculine—think soldiers, police offices, manual labourers, and drivers. Ta's are almost certainly married to women. Meti men are submissive with feminine traits, yet they are still expected to marry women and they aren't seen as gay or trans within Nepali language or society.

My friend and I had known Ravi for a few weeks. Out of drag, Ravi was a quiet and serious faced counsellor at the Blue Diamond Society, Nepal's only LGBTQIA+ centre at the time. Rani was completely different; mesmerising, enigmatic, mysterious, and able to command the attention of everyone in her vicinity.

Ravi identified as gay and was not overtly femme. He wasn't trans and didn't have a burning desire to dress in drag. This was unlike many of his friends, who asked us in fevered whispers if it was true that in Western countries people underwent surgery and were able to take hormones. Was it true, they asked, that if they took whole packets of the contraceptive pill that they would grow breasts?

Ravi performed the role of a meti so that he could go out and meet men, have sex, and be accepted, if only for a brief moment, in Nepali society. Ravi told me that the only way he could be accepted as a gay man in Nepal was if he was seen as a ta. At the time, this stance was startling to me. I couldn't understand why he wanted to perform femininity to that extent if it wasn't who he felt himself to be. When he was in drag as Rani, he embodied the character. He was her, surely?

But now, many years later, I am not as confused. So much has changed, including our understanding of queer identities, within the English language. Maybe we are all cross dressers—trying on different identities throughout our lives and discarding other pieces of ourselves. In the words of the most famous drag queen in the world, RuPaul, 'we are all born naked, and the rest is drag.'

In Kathmandu, I was the one with a limited view, thinking that dressing in drag made Rani trans or gender fluid. No, Rani was simply a part of Ravi, a character he played and a mask he wore when he felt like entering a certain world. I was the one that didn't have the language to understand this at the time.

We stood on the darkened street in Kathmandu, the compact dirt under our ill-fitting heels, the folds of the sari foreign against our skin. We waited for Rani outside the entrance of the nightclub, the throbbing music pulsing through our bodies.

Within minutes she was back, striding triumphantly around the corner and out of the shadows.

With a wobble of her head she uttered one word.

'Jannu.'

With that, we followed her across the threshold eagerly.

New Haunts

Emma Ashmere

I'm back in my old country from the old countries with its parrot-coloured money and a sky not needing another adjective flung at it. From the hostel window, freedom unrecognised.

Too broke for a plane back east so it's a bus trip for two days and nights cushioned against a large soft woman who offers me large soft food. Stare out at the flat the grey green orange following us behind large soft windows. Roadhouse in the middle of somewhere. Another passenger hands me a joint. Stretch the legs, back, arms, shrink the mind.

Dawn. The driver stops says everyone get out and look. We squint along arching ochre layers of cliffs of the Bight. The sea-heave rises inside of me. Thanks, we shout. The wind sweeps our words in the direction of almost home.

This is my parents' new townhouse with the Australian flag. They are narrower. Their accents wider. Tears tea wine beer cheese n' jatz. We sidle-stagger through lost years of furniture and perch on small topics, TV shows I've never watched, people friends family strangers who've lived and died. I add my glass and cup to the two clean cups stacked in the sink. Two spoons. Two plates. I roll out my sleeping bag which still smells of Her beneath the fold-away dining table waiting for collapse.

I'm moving to Melbourne next week says my only Adelaide friend.

We drive straight roads to the Exeter Hotel and dock outside its chewing gum glittering milky way pavement, my feet unused to gravity, we push on the airlocked pub door to find faces invented or remembered preserved in smoke.

Your hair says Friend.

I left it in London.

Jittery cold. I should be inured from cold and loss. Friend lends me a flanny shirt which smells like the back of her car and a beret for old time's sake. Remember back when we both came out, Friend says, back when we rode our bikes through the back streets to The Exeter Hotel, back when called it The Exciter, and we called going out dealing at The Austral Hotel Going Up The Nostril, back when we thought the world would see all of its mistakes.

I nod her beret to make her smile.

A band sprouts loud in the beer garden. Possibly the same band there always was. Possibly not. Stand by the salt-damp courtyard wall. Do I know this stunted tree does it know me with its sharp bits prodding my restless back the smoke of kreteks dope booze plumbing planning with Her standing in front of me very close too close for public not close enough, planning our escape.

You should meet This One, says Friend making her way to me through the music. Say cheese when she comes over.

This One she call her. This One has hair of spiked rose, is a film student and has a new job cooking for a catering company at the back of a cheese shop. Don't look at her eyes. Her boss is advertising for someone to work for a two month stint film shoot long hours haughty actors stressed directors lousy pay scenery changeable pathway to anywhere questionable.

I'm looking for work, I say to the face sliding about in my beer. Looking for everything.

At the Cheese Shop my mind is a trailer of should-have-been-deleted scenes. I try to listen as This One and I are apprenticed in the art of cooking roulades by our energetic boss. Turns out roulades are just omelettes viewed from another angle rolled and stuffed with cheesey herby fillings miscellaneous. The Cheese Shop bell rings. I stand at the glass counter where customers lean and breathe and point and say not that one this one no I want that larger no a smaller piece without the rind or maybe with it but is that what people prefer for a platter and are you sure it is if fresh hang on can I taste a bit first and hang on now I need a bigger bit I can't decide, as I, the tour guide lead them through valleys and dells of curds and whey labelled with goats Swiss bells and belles and French and Italian words cut in half.

Our boss has high permanently surprised pencilled-in eyebrows and whisks nouns into verbs with a dash of DIY adverbery. Plate it down consildatarily she says creating a new word and another empty space in a roulade-gridlocked freezer.

This One and I graduate from roulades to spanikopitas. Fold butter fill cut fold butter.

The secret is to mint and to oregano the mixture with liberalitly says the boss. Don't waste the spinach stems finely chopped The Greeks eat the lot.

I don't say I've eaten the real thing in Rhodes squinting up to see the Colossus standing where he no longer stood with Her caught in an off the map war zone, no visitors allowed. I don't say Her and I was a mistake. That I should have known we were just flirter traveller companion friends-or-faux.

Her was always a stranger, even more so when we rattled up to the ancestors' village Her saying no it will be fine, they'll love you, don't worry, and I knew it wouldn't be as soon as we hauled our backpacks off the bus high in the pine-haze mountains, glimmer dust mote bright, armies of old women hugging Her, asking when she was getting married to some name some character I'd never heard of, or so she confessed later.

Her laughing talking in language I didn't understand, and I didn't mind, catching my eye with meanings I understood, me retreating, lying on a bed of stone in a hut hacked into a hill, standing alone at the tiny white-washed window watching Her walk those floured roads with Her great aunts and grandmothers and old second third cousins every dusk, until I couldn't see which one was Her, their black-stockinged legs bandy-curved parentheses swollen hands lighting a candle every day for their dead husbands' bones soon to descend to the ossuary, all the women carrying their flowers and herbs and sorrows dodging the spitfire caterpillars swarming in the trees stepping over the slivers of glittering shattered headlights dead tourists marked with plastic flowers and locals with cairns of stone. Now run your fingers over the bullet holes in the old church walls, Her said, after dancing all night at somebody's wedding, hear that cracking? Did they guess?

Me coming in at night after talking to sunburnt English tourists in a bar and not finding Her, just a torn faded floured map I couldn't read flung on the bed.

Up early. Cheese Shop boss's red cheese truck thrums outside my parents' townhouse. Rushed tea and buttered bread for them, porridge for me shaky-spooned from a cold ceramic cup cradled on my borrowed Friend's flanny shirt, slide in beside with This One, This New One, This Possible One, This Don't Even Think About It, This One I Thought Of All The Night.

The boss noun-verbs at the wheel eyebrows high in a high red cabin grinding up hairpin hills past the cat and dog home that no longer exists.

I whisper to This One but you can still hear the barks and meows and how-dare-yous and she laughs, a small fire rising inside of me as we labour around the Devil's Elbow once alight in memory, or am I rewriting and embellishing. Does This One remember and was she living here back then when that conflagration aflame electric radiator orange dragon landed and ate the surrounding hills.

Remember the imported eagle impersonating a church lectern, This One says.

Or maybe I said it and she smiles.

We judder through memories and forgetting and the ambush of possibilities that may or may not make the final cut, through the mock unEnglish orchards and yellow green fields paddocks meadows, or perhaps they're not real, afterimages imprinted on my eyes along with the smoke machine smog and wind-machine politics of all gone London where I fled with Her when the ancestors saw us, spied on us I said, which Her denied. I'm thinking of those orange chimney pots we watched change their colour in Battersea snow and sleet and moonless nights that fell at three in the afternoon, shivering in Her fold down attic bed, when at last I could see her face, and see her coming back to me, no longer the colour of unreadable maps and unknowable histories. Me waving a plane ticket.

Now I'm here with This One's filmic thigh pressed against mine in the front seat of a truck. Do I dare turn, pan upwards, or say no don't, pull back, wide shot, fade to bright, feel her hand against mine, blink shut your eyes past beautiful granite boulders spray-painted with i was here so-and-so forever and ND is a slut voices hissing in the grass. Open your eyes.

We're here, she says.

We're waved into a small city of tents and vans and white portable everythings and people with clipboards and important hair and strides of purposeful impatience and expensive precision. I can feel This One's thigh-print warmth blossoming expanding as we unload the truck and unfold the tables the cookers and gas bottles. There's no fridge because the boss can't outlay for a refrigerated vehicle because her other car, a black soft top BMW, is only leased for the duration of the shoot so the film people'll think she's rich like all film people are apparently, and she can't risk losing the contract if they find out she's really struggling to pay the import taxes on her cheeses because life is all about appearances if you want to get a head or a leg up or a hand up or any part of your anatomy over the parapet.

So it's a busy conga line of eskies disgorging roulades as we step over Medusa's version of electric cords crisscrossing our unfilmed world and unleash pre-washed rockets for salads and saw roulades into snail-rounds keep stop washing up faster and faster until someone says quiet will you all quiet camera action and somebody consults the light-meter and the continuity woman curses the fickledom of clouds.

I laugh silently when the continuity woman shakes a fist at a plane rumbling over the already adjective-cluttered sky.

Morning tea. Lunch. Afternoon tea.

We don't dare look at each other when the lead actor demands special reactions and recognitions and special dressing for the salad rocketed asap to the special dressing room which is only a hired caravan with frilly curtains drenched in spray-can lavender.

I say to This One I want to be the continuity woman. How about you?

The director of course.

Tomorrow, truck idling, peach dawn matches her rosey hair in the salted air, the sea flat and silvered with similes, sand squeaking, bleached beaches of youth, and crowds, look at those crowds suddenly camped in the dunes with cameras trained on us thinking we're somebody.

This One and I are asked to be extras walking stumbling flying along the beach pointing at something neither of us can see.

Lower my hand. Brush it against hers.

Cut.

Tomorrow and tomorrow, serving roulades on a pretty hill, city street, posh house with swimming pool, poor house with weeds, restaurant, prison, hotel, fern house.

After plating up and plating down we become extras again.

Action, too late. We forget to take off our aprons, and try not to scream to shout to holler at a silent car bursting into silent flames rolling down a silent hill.

Her finger curls around mine.

Back at the shop. Night. Dishes. No boss. Just us. Just four washing-up gloved hands plunging into soupy sinks.

She's smiling at me.

Is this in the script?

She takes my hand, frees it, takes me to her car to her sharehouse to her bed to her life.

*

Another Good Thing You Can Do When You Have Fire

Alli Sebastian Wolf

Sharlet's bicycle was feeling too classical music today. Not like specific classical, not Chopin or anything. Just general classical. It has been since she replaced the spokes with harp strings. It's the playing card that does it - the rapid-fire tickticktick replaced with delicate tickles and she feels like she should be dressed in gossamer.

Sharlet is not really sure what gossamer is and anyway she is not dressed in it. She's wearing ripped jeans and a faded black shirt with a pterodactyl on the front and cuts across the back so when she leans forward to peddle you get a small glimpse of un-bra'd side boob. Or you could if she wasn't going so fast, leaving the trailing sound of a baroque banquet in her wake.

She gets to Deni's via the dentist's backyard to steal an apple from under the possum netting. He hears slow harp plucking as she wheels her bike under his window, and he thinks the stoners next door have finally acquired some taste.

Letting her bike fall with tinkling discord where she skidded on the driveway gravel, Sharlet throws the apple into Deni's window.

Then her friend is at the door, half smile of suppressing a huge grin and a half-eaten apple spinning from her hand.

Sharlet catches it, it's sweet and cold, and she wipes juice from her chin.

'Ready?'

Deni has a regular bike, bright orange like toxic waste but no strange sounds or powers, not even those fluoro plastic toggles that clack up and down the spokes. Though this bike once saw Frank Zappa walking a ferret years after they said he had died, Deni wasn't there, and the bike hasn't said anything – it is pretty much an ordinary bike.

Deni is not ordinary.

Her cloak is loose to cover her wings. She attached them with fencing wire yesterday and today they are trying them out.

She did not sleep well, the corners dug in to her skin.

'You should have taken them off,' Sharlet tells her.

That would not be taking this seriously, Deni knows, and these girls are taking this seriously.

'You sound like a fairy princess,' Deni yells over the strings beside her.

'Fairy princesses are badass.'

Deni doesn't disagree with the girl in the ripped pterodactyl shirt. She is riding alongside her fast enough to see the sides of small breasts and soft flesh over ribs. She is enchanted and keeps watching Sharlet's lips, knowing they taste apple-sweet like hers. Her wings hurt, jabbing into her back over potholes. She doesn't say anything. Sharlet is going to be so impressed.

They are heading to Black Mountain. Black mountain is more of a large hill but it looms blackly over the town because of all the bare slate. Nothing that dark and jagged should be called a hill so the residents named it 'Mountain' and then built their houses facing the other way.

Respect and acceptance are different things.

'You sound like a fairy princess,' Deni says again, though she is the one with the wings on under her cloak.

'Badass,' repeats Sharlet and Deni realises she was hoping Sharlet would notice the irony and say that about her.

Sharlet speeds up and the harp strings turn into a high hum like the vibration in a b-movie *Kung Fu* temple. Deni is thinking about little levitating bald men when Sharlet rounds the corner and disappears.

She tucks her hair into her cloak and becomes an orange blur – these girls can ride.

At the top of the mountain they look down over the whole town – its backs all turned on them. But these girls are used to that – and the height and scale of the mountain make them feel powerful. They feel an affinity with this mountain of metamorphic rock. What the mountain feels is unknown. It saw Zappa that day too but has never mentioned it. Its days of heat and passion are done.

The girls' bikes are nestled against a tree like nuzzling horses, Deni's gut turns.

'Now?' asks Sharlet.

'Now.' And the cloak flutters to the ground.

She runs, magnificent,

wings unfolding like a giant condor.

All metal and leather and speed.

They rattle in the wind and she feels lift

She feels power

Reaches the edge and jumps

And feels the ground of the rock shelf below.

Sharlet is jumping down to her.

'The leather is too heavy.' She reaches her friend and untangles her from the wingy mess.

Deni checks that she is not broken. Grazes from the landing, piercings from the fencing wire. Not much blood.

'Bamboo and nylon -' Sharlet goes on.

'It has to be skin.' They've had this argument already. Deni will not be shifted. Certainly not with her ankle hurting like this. Ask if I'm alright, Sharlet. 'No plastic - it has to be me.'

Sharlet does not argue, and does not ask how she is.

Sharlet knows how she is. Sharlet knows a lot about her. Almost everything.

She knows once Deni gets the mix right the wings will fuse into her and they will be hers as if she were born with them. She knows this more than Deni does because she remembers how Deni got a tail in year three, and no university savings were spent on a parade of surgeons and psychiatrists to convince Sharlet otherwise. After that Deni is not as sure as she thinks she is.

And Sharlet is not sure if she will be left when her only friend can fly away.

She doesn't ask how Deni is.

But she folds the wings carefully and helps her up the rocks.

They sit looking over the small backs to them town, full of small-town people with small backs to their ideas. It looks quiet.

'I don't like that place,' Deni says.

'No.'

She seems sad, Deni thinks. Disappointed even.

Deni wants to tell her that she will do better, that Sharlet is beautiful and will not be let down, but rubs her ankle and instead says 'You want me to stop?' Fishing again.

Sharlet is holding the wings and looking at her softly, she looks out at the town, or maybe the sky just above it – Deni can't tell – then back at her and holds out the wings.

'I want to be amazed.' She says.

'Okay.' And Deni kicks off from the rock and jumps through time.

Deni has been able to jump between times for around six months now, she discovered it accidentally and didn't seem to have any control over the timing – short jumps into the imitate future.

It was a secret - she had wanted to save it for some last minute saving the day or something, once she'd figured out how to use it properly, but Sharlet seemed so disappointed and she wanted desperately to impress her – the fearless girl who bit the dog that scared Deni when they were five, who made her a tail, fought off anyone who teased them with pretend kung fu moves, spelt her name to be like shark and could replace her spokes with harp strings.

So Deni jumped through time.

But it doesn't feel right - maybe she had just given away her ace too soon and now Sharlet would never fall in love with her.

When she lands seconds later it is dark on the mountain hill and Sharlet has started a fire.

She is wrapped in Deni's cloak, burning little pinecones which spit and hiss. The dancing of the flames make the shadows of their bikes waltz. She doesn't look up.

Deni's thinks she looks beautiful in the firelight, like a Celtic goddess, but Sharlet's expression stops her from saying anything and she just sits down beside her.

On their mountain hill, not touching, or talking,
or looking at anything.
They sit for a long time.

Sharlet takes out her lighter and puts it away
again.

Then Deni notices remains of her wings in the fire.

And Sharlet is crying.

The night stretches ...

Deni remembers an orange from her cloak, 'Remember this?' she squeezes the rind into the fire making crackling yellow flames. She knows Sharlet remembers, Sharlet taught her how not to get your fingers burnt doing it.

But it makes her smile.

And then it is just the two of them again, huddled under a cloak by the fire on Black Mountain, watching the glowing caterpillars of freight trains in the distance and licking orange juice from their wrists.

Holding hands in the darkness.

'Another thing you can do with fire ...' Sharlet turns a stick in the embers.

The girls look down at the tiny town. 'Burn it?'

'Burn it.'

So they did.

THE END

Cannibals

Tanya Vavilova

After my wife Lucy died, I started going to Bondi Icebergs once a week. I'd sit in the sauna in my old one-piece and eavesdrop on the talk of others: chunky men, girls in string bikinis, young mums. I'd steam, then dive into the icy pool, then steam, then dive into the icy pool. Not that I believed in the health benefits—the studio was just full of Lucy's clothes and art; it was nice to get away from it.

After a while, I got to know the Wednesday regulars. We'd nod in recognition. Give a shy wave. The two balding men who sat by the stove liked to bring up the moon landing. I think they were Russian or maybe Polish. Their accents were thick like soup. The small, pinched woman in the corner, Suzanne, liked to complain to her friend about the council. 'The autumn leaves are piling up,' she said one chilly morning. 'Someone will slip, crack their skull.'

Lucy had died in a freak accident: run over by a golf buggy. No one was held responsible. When I told Suzanne about it, she gave me the phone number of her psychiatrist. I took that to mean she cared.

I loved Wednesdays at the sauna. Loved the regulars. The ritual soothed some of the pain.

One Wednesday in April, however, I had to stay home and wait for a delivery from the funeral home. By the time the package arrived, it was almost five o'clock—I lit a candle for Lucy and ordered pizza. I tipped her ashes into a vintage Arnott's tin and put it on the mantel next to a ceramic duck . It was good to have her back.

The next morning, a Thursday, as soon as I opened the sauna door, I knew something was up. I didn't recognise anyone. I mean, chunky men, girls in string bikinis, mums, they were all there, but they were not my chunky men, my girls in bikinis, my mums.

A girl with hoop earrings sneered as I took my usual place on the top rung. After about two minutes, I found it hard to breathe. Who were these people? They were loud and sweaty. Someone like Suzanne described Sculpture by the Sea as 'plebeian.' There was talk of some café serving Single Origin. I slumped down the steps, first one then two. Then I was on the floor. It was hard to swallow.

People came and went, more chunky men, more girls, more mums. The shuffle of new people meant no one knew how long I'd been lying there for. They stepped right over me.

Someone kicked my shin.

Soon, I was broiling like a chicken. I was probably dead.

Near closing time, I noticed people eyeing each other. They were staring at my fleshy thighs with hunger. A bro glanced out the tiny window before bending down and snapping off my leg. 'Not bad,' he said taking a bite, before passing my calf to his mate. 'Tastes like chicken.'

Soon, more people were leaning over me, tearing off my hands and feet. A brute with a swiss army knife cut off my shoulder and passed it around. People took a bite.

Soon, all that was left was my head, and someone swung open the door and kicked it like a beachball into the pool.

I thought of Lucy and my Wednesday regulars as I bobbed in the water, kids chucking cold chips at my head.

The Goddess of Ritual Madness

Lydia Trethewey

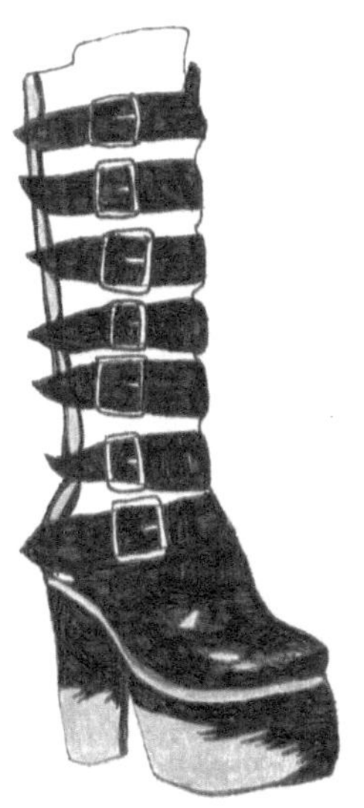

1.

The boots are acid green and tear thin films from my heels. I wear them every day regardless, marching through the city. I keep buying fluorescent fishnet bodysuits and PVC skirts, hoodies with shoulder spikes denim jackets cheap trash and enamel pins. Before, I would never have thought this was me, but now it's urgent, necessary, I'm dying for goth platforms and plastic pasties, a surgical reinvigoration of my closet.

I am the goddess of ritual madness.

At the end of each week, I weep over my bank account, chew down my nails and reiterate again, that I need this, I need this new me.

2.

Sometimes I'm not going anywhere, just walking in my new skin and eating greasy chips from the station, sitting outside the state library wondering how I ever chewed through all this time. People glance as they pass and say *nice boots* or else furrow their brows distastefully thinking *what fucking ugly boots* but the point is, they can't help but notice, so I win. I wander circuitously like hours sweating and when I return the apartment is tired and slicked-down from my having nowhere to be. Sometimes weeks have passed or no time at all.

Treadmill days.

3.

Queer time moves differently, it's like a salsa or a waltz, like sea-salt waves that reiterate, each step unwinds and rebirths the next, or less charitably, this is my second adolescence. I've heard trans people call it that though this isn't the same, and the girls on *Her* say I'm a twenty-six-year-old baby gay. I'm not in control of the terminology but then I'm not in control of anything, it seems.

Renaissance is the French word for rebirth, but there are no philosophers to muse on my nascent embryology.

4.

After wasting myself all week, I peel off the sequined crop-top and fling it into the clamshell suitcase, I collapse onto my friend's couch, he's at work, his apartment smells of bird dirt and dried corn. Poetry books and unwashed socks, and below it all is my laptop, a forum full of late bloomers and guilt and memes.

People keep telling me I'd change my mind if I found the right cock. The word *Lesbian* feels pornographic. We married just after high school, he knows I'm "bisexual" but he keeps making homophobic comments. I think he knows. I'm insecure about my lack of experience. *Lesbian Gym: the story of a virgin who was seduced into the wrong kind of loving.*

5.

Time moves both frenetic and sluggish when you're divorced at twenty-six, I'm exhausted and dislocated from the normal trajectory, having all my parts severed and packaged up to be sold into a brave new commodity culture. Rainbow capitalism pink tax have I read enough queer theory to be properly out.

A dream where ugly men in suits surround my naked corpse drawing red lipstick lines across my flesh deciding the best cuts, butcher-shop fantasy I came in my sleep and then woke up crying.

Disarticulated, I can't speak the right words, I have sex with internet strangers, pussy slime all over my lips. Sleeping on the couch of some cockatiel-obsessed acquaintance I don't remember meeting.

6.

Apollo looks at me with eyes knit when I rock up to her house in my new kink-fashion; my expression askew from rough dreams. Her fiancé Timothy averts his eyes and a blush creeps into the room, he's stuttering, H-h-hi, D, did you want some dinner? He's got a roast chicken and the peas are boiling over.

Apollo has her arms folded, she scours the thinness of me scrubs me clean with her gaze and I grin, I say I already ate, she says is that a joke I don't get? Probably, but she asks if I wouldn't rather sleep in their guest room than on a rando's couch, feel settled, but I don't accept the offer because she's Apollo and I'm Dionysius.

Peas bouncing up and down in the water, involuntarily I think of Tim's testes in his ball sack rising and falling like the cremaster cycle. It's almost summer again. I shred the velvet of my antlers or tip the velvet of my ancestors.

7.

I don't know which parts of me are relevant anymore, but I've got my boots on so I go to the station and there's this artsy queer porn thing playing in the gallery tonight, second floor above the paper-swept street, above the café that sells vegan raw foods in Northbridge where bogans drink themselves out of existence.

Sticky veins in Transperth carpet Apollo's concern is a bur stuck in my exposed throat, a drunk leers at me as the train disappears into evening. We all sway on altered gravity. I'm a hedonistic animal, succumbing to the inevitable.

8.

Posters on the walls, I'm intoxicated on film-reel bodies unravelling, the light touches women's wetness to my lips. I grin and suck in all her experience, slurping. There's a demonstration of dominance. Hypnotism it bores me I tap my boots against the floor. I lose time again the movies are made of sinews and filaments, fingers and honey and lubricated coke bottles exploding and the audience cheers.

I need to belong here, because here is all that's left.

I stumble back to the apartment, restlessness making nests behind my eyelids, little spider legs itching at the parts of me which refuse to fall asleep.

9.

Queer temporality is a never-ending recursion, I repeat my story every few days: yes, I'm a lesbian, yes, I moved in with a friend, I don't know, of course my husband knows, how could he not?

Divorce. I don't know. I don't know. You'd have to ask him.

My housemate's bird dive-bombs and craps on us from above, watching with beady-eyed awareness the realisation that I shouldn't be here. Apollo comes to check on me. We represent different periods of history, she and I, cycles, I converse with the memory of my married life.

10.

I'm 34, no kids, married for fifteen years, I can't believe I didn't know, it's not like I'm from a conservative religious family or live in a repressive country, I have no excuse. I'm 25, have been out as bi for years but after my last break up (with a man) I think I might be gay, mistaking comphet for attraction. Is it normal to feel nervous when naked? We've been conditioned to expect so little from men, we don't notice when it's actually nothing. Gay men discover their homosexuality on average four years earlier than gay women. He told me that bisexuality was the default for girls, and that we're naturally more affectionate with each other. Cuddle buddies they're just good friends, gal pals roommates we can't apply our contemporary notions of homosexuality to the past (though we can when they're straight).

11.

Then there's E. At the goth night I'm supposed to meet E outside the club but she bails, so I'm standing here in tar makeup not knowing how to dance, sinking, my inner ear is out of alignment I feel sick in the vertigo music I've spent my whole life waiting.

She shows up later, in my dreams, holding a collar.

In the queer community, everyone belongs to everyone. Don't be a prude.

12.

Apollo calls and her voice disrupts my unbalanced cochlea, compress and expand me I'm ironed out and tired Are you happy she asks me and no, I'm not anything much but clothes and odd decisions happiness is temporary and queer temporality goes on and on indefinitely. I fill in the gaps in my life the synapses re-forming it's not that I missed out on expressing myself, I missed out on being myself.

Butler says there's no identity behind expression, there's only doing not being, but maybe she needed to suck more dick to understand that not everyone can flick a switch between sexual proclivities, and I want to ask, are virgins still allowed to be gay?

I have this blank page and a pen balanced on the web of skin between my thumb and forefinger, I have thoughts but I'm on mute, dumb animal how did I end up here, words are just breath but immortal or whatever, I put the paper away and open my computer.

13.

E never laughs but I know she smiles when I can't see, when I'm on my forearms and knees dolphin pose and she's arranging me like a piece of prose, her softness is hard, she bites sometimes and I cry, her wrists are mottled with the gristle of self-harm.

She's messaging me, wants to meet up but not in a club, in a park. Wants to stroke my back in the sun like a cat and take me home and take care of me. She says, I wanna get a nice fat dildo that attaches to the floor and you're gonna ride that dick like the whore you are, she says, I want to see you arch that back take it deep grunt and moan, TV shows are boring you're going to be my own personal porn channel, I'll train you to perform how I want.

I'm 27, I've been married for six and a half years, together with my husband for nine, we have two young children. About a year ago I felt a sudden surge of attraction for my lesbian co-worker, we work in an office, we've been constantly flirting since, I feel like I terrible person, but I've also never felt so much like myself.

14.

Artificial exhaustion, I want to be in love at least once before I die. One of my enamel pins is shaped like a name tag, the words Hi, I'm a bad idea, printed on and another is a luna moth, green wings folded across my chest. Luna moths spend most their lives underground, but when they come out they fuck continuously until they die.

I wear my denim jacket to the park but E doesn't notice the pin, she says, wow, those boots are hard to miss and I miss an opportunity to explain that I'm more than just a costume, we sit on a bench by the lake and she sees my book, asks me what I'm reading, and I show her the cover, it was the first story published in Serbia with an openly lesbian protagonist, but it doesn't end well, her name is the same as mine just different spelling, and E says, I still don't know what your real name is.

Would you like to know? No.

A Morton Bay Fig spits seeds all over the concrete, E spreads a shagged purple blanket out on the grass and I take my boots off.

15.

One day I can feel myself disappearing so I Google my own name, but I'm not there, a potato researcher in Texas has stolen my identity so I spend the afternoon reading his papers on heterologous expression of keto hexokinase in abnormal leaf development and the signal transduction pathways controlling in planta tuberization.

Hi, I'm a Bad Idea.

16.

There's a cat on E's bed but he scrambles off as we fall and I'm wearing the same crop-top, unwashed, basically a bra with black plastic buckles like an airplane seatbelt and E unclips them peels the fabric away. You've got such beautiful tits (they always seem to say).

Is that what women think I want to hear, am I making up for something other than time?

She licks my nipples bites sharp pain sprouting through my skin a pit of tar in which we sink, shhh baby girl, stay still, and I think, did you know that mastodons not mammoths were the original furry elephant beasts, and that etymologically "mastodon" means nipple-teeth? E makes me stand naked in the corner while she masturbates and we do not speak.

17.

My husband realised first, connected my confusion to all the absent pieces like our sexless marriage and my distaste at holding hands in public, he kicked me out before I'd even come to a conclusion, I think we can be friends again though, in the future. When I told my husband, he didn't believe me, he's so great but we're like roommates, is this just what married life is like? I feel so empty. As a kid, I used to cut out lingerie models from magazines and keep them under my bed. I felt nervous singing the male part in songs, because people might think I was gay. I didn't understand what the deal was with fingernails. Big tittie goth girl memes about WLW always centring on top-bottom crocodile death roll you should watch this show it has lesbians in it. When a guy sleeps with lots of girls he's a "player" but when I do it, I'm a "lesbian".

18.

E messages me and her stream of consciousness is a psycho-sexual heliography, her anodyne sins spilled into words like a vomitorium. I'm going to keep you bruised, baby girl, when you pull down your pants and sit on the toilet and look down you'll see yourself covered in my beautiful marks like ocean flowers you'll know I own you I want to smack your pussy make her red you're my slut you better make sure you lick and suck that dildo a lot cos next you're riding it with your tight little ass and you ain't getting no lube.

The word Homophilia sounds wrong, perverted, though it centres love over sex. If such terminology were still in vogue, would we continue to speak of homoromantic asexuality? So much is just getting the words right, trying them on like tight pants to see which fits, I was a lesbian in category before in practice, Butler.

Gay and straight are not eternal, a science of identity but to define is to limit and coming out is a political act taken in the street.

19.

My heels have scabbed over and now I walk with ease, stride through Northbridge like I'm following a script, Wednesday night there's live lesbian mud wrestling and I've never been but when I arrive at the club my feet shiver with a new calloused freedom and I want to leave. I want to go to the book store and sift through thin poetry spines and buy far too many, walk home with them gathered in my arms and I kind of want to descend the piss-soaked stairwell in the car park and find a woman in a public bathroom and put my tongue between her legs. I'm inherently deviant queer and in the book shop volumes of BDSM and kink are kept beside lesbian self-help veneer.

Sacher-Masoch lived his life as if it were fiction, masochism is a lived fiction he manipulated reality he wasn't a victim am I living or am I gathering material to write with?

20.

There are more plastic pens rolling around the bottom of my bag than there are thoughts in my head, and the presence of one amplifies the absence of the other, little bits of dross litter my peace. Orwell thought writing was like thinking but I maintain it's like puking, a sudden and violent ejection which leaves you feeling sick for hours after.

Hours or days, this new freedom is an exaggerated temporality I struggle to fill, coming out has emptied my past of relevance, I can't find myself there. Haunted by the tacit antiquity of past queerness ignored.

A zoo soap opera: gay penguins steal nest with eggs from lesbian couple. High school stoning: when I was fifteen, my friend told me she liked me, but after I came out she called me a predator and they all threw rocks. Useless lesbians: I want to ask her out, but I can't. In 2004 the children's show *Play School* featured a segment with lesbian parents, and the Prime Minister felt the need to declare that children should be protected from such harmful rhetoric. If we show gay couples on TV, the straight kids might get confused. If we show heterosexual couples on TV, the gay kids might get confused, but nobody gives a shit. Comphet like a soviet aesthetic for lesbian feminism, I trawl through other people's stories thinking I might find myself somewhere.

21.

I'm thirty-eight and I came out to my husband a month ago, he wants us to stay together, because he has a lesbian fetish. I can never tell my husband, because he's a homophobe, and I don't know what he'd do. I can't believe I did this to him. I kissed a woman for the first time today, and it felt amazing.

22.

At a party with E, there's a ball pit and free pot, a woman with short hair and long legs I wonder what it would feel like to love her, I need a place to set my love.

E and I pant in summer heat and my excitement is punctured with discomfort, I can't figure it out, there's not a single species in the world that reproduces sexually in which homosexual behaviour has not been observed. Yet a photograph of two lions stacked in the African savanna rubbing manes and rutting is captioned "social bonding". I want to bond with as many women as possible to legitimise myself, if Butler's right and homosexuality is about practice not identity, I can't sit still, but I keep thinking if I'm not attracted to this specific woman does that mean I'm not really gay? If I take a day off, does my sexuality cease to exist? I'm not a masochist when I'm washing the dishes. I get whiplash trying to see everything that's happening.

23.

Crying on the phone to Apollo, I don't know what I am anymore, this search has swallowed me and I can't even understand what I need, and she asks me, are you a hedonist, of course, of course I am, now, and probably before, too, she strokes my flattened ego and says, hedonism isn't having orgies and getting drunk, or being a slave to your passions, it's the philosophy of life in which you only do what you want. See? The important part is that you know what you want. Tell me, what do you really want?

I want to be in love at least once before I die.

I can no longer stand on the past to reach the future.

Dionysius is the god responsible for epiphanies.

Farewell to The Witches

Emily James

Your shaky car pulls up on the uneven road halfway between two houses. You pull up the handbrake, which lets out a sigh of relief, or a shudder. You can't quite tell.

There's a churning in your stomach. Hunger – or anxiety? Each time you come back these feelings become more difficult to identify.

There are mixed feelings about this place, this visit, these people. There always have been. You feel them swirl and stick in your stomach, a bubbling concoction. A witch's brew. Even now, with ten years since you last lived here, you still feel unsettled. Unable to fit in.

You attempt to dismiss the uneasiness with a quick exhale as you get out of the car. Locking it hesitantly, you catch your reflection in the side window just before you turn around. A denim jacket hangs off your narrow shoulders, the bottom gently caressing a tired leather belt wearily holding up thrifted khaki pants. You peer into your car's backseat for anything that could inject some form of femininity into your appearance. Nothing. You sigh and lock your door.

Walking up the trampled, uneven driveway, you glance up at the row of birds perched on the powerlines, peering down at you with daggers of disapproval. Like elderly relatives or concerned neighbours, hinting at the disappointed looks you'll be met with when you reach the door.

You had neighbours of the concerning kind all those years ago, your parents were the concerned ones, though. Loud neighbours, too quiet neighbours, neighbours with obnoxious children that no child of mine would never be seen hanging around with, understood? You remember those neighbours.

But none came close in your family's eyes —perhaps the whole street's eyes—to the neighbours in the house adjacent to yours. You knew them well, but only through mutters, snickers, the occasional jeer yelled from a car driving past or a child who was too stupid to be scared.

The Witches. Two of them, childless and nameless, they moved in next door when you were only young. You remember the day they arrived, when your mother shook her head, saying she'd pray they wouldn't stay long. "We don't want to be living near that kind," she snarled.

An intolerable memory floods into your mind. You forget that you're still standing in the driveway staring at The Witches' House just like you were a few months after you lost your paper aeroplane, all those years ago. You were playing alone when you heard a cry from inside their house, like someone had been frightened or hurt. Disturbed at least. Frantic footsteps began sounding from one of their open windows - smaller, nimble footsteps followed by heavier ones, desperate to keep up. You dived behind a bin and froze with fear and fascination. Who, or what, had dared to disturb The Witches?

George Michaels, it seemed. The Least-Well-Behaved Boy on the block shoved open the flyscreen door and broke into a sprint. His face was horribly white, as if he had painted the stark colour on. He looked like a clown. Your mother always called him a clown, said he was always joking or laughing about something. He was certainly not laughing now.

Tall Witch bolted after him with supernatural speed. She grabbed his arm, fingers like talons digging into prey and he yelped with pain and fear.

"Now you listen to me," she hissed as they came to a halt. "You're not to tell anyone about this. Not anyone, you understand?"

"L-let me go," George stuttered. George Michaels never stuttered. He snickered, he snarled, but he never stuttered. He was trembling, and as you looked to Tall Witch, you saw she was too.

"You promise me you won't say anything. Promise me!" she cried, beginning to shake as if startled by the volume and desperation of her own voice. She was terrified.

But what of?

George and Tall Witch stared at each other as seconds went by, both paralysed by fear. George was only growing paler. Tall Witch released her grip, only slightly, but it was enough. He tore free and sprinted down the side path onto the street, fringe failing to mask the stream of tears that ran down his cheeks.

"Katie!" a shrill voice cries from the front door, making George and Tall Witch disappear as your jolted back to the present. You whip your head around to spot your mother, shoulders hunched, slender, almost sickly stature tense as ever, squinting at you from the veranda. She always sounds like a screeching bird when she's irritated. Which she always is.

"What's the matter with you? You've been standing in the driveway for about two minutes," she retorts.

You shake your head, scattering the memories far and wide. "Nothing mum, I'm fine."

She snorts. "Don't know what's so interesting about Tall and Tubby's. That old dump's been the same for twenty years. Now get inside," she says with urgency, as if she's smuggling you in, still shielding you from The Witches next door.

She's still afraid of them. Tall Witch and Tubby Witch – the two wicked women who tried something sinister with George Michaels. For at least a year after it happened you were convinced they were trying to eat him. Boil him up in a stew like Tubby Witch would've done to you. When you stopped believing that, you thought he must have tried and failed to prank them, perhaps. And after that, you tried not to think about him, them and home too much at all.

You finally go inside, walking briskly down the narrow hallway into your mother's makeshift interrogation room – the kitchen.

Why haven't you come back in so long? Why do you come back so much, surely you should be trying to get some more work? What on earth do you think you're wearing? You used to look so lovely in the dresses and skirts I'd make you; the whole street would say how jealous they were not to have such a nice young lady for a daughter.

"Have you got a boyfriend?"

The question still makes your body stiffen with discomfort and your voice strain with anxiety.

"No, Mum, I don't have time."

"Don't have time?" She sighs, turning away to attack the kitchen table by vigorously scrubbing it with a worn rag.

"Speaking of Tall and Tubby, they're leaving."

"Leaving?" You almost feel your ears prick up, like a dog hearing its owner's keys in the door. "Where to? For how long?"

"Oh, they're moving out. Leaving for good, I mean," your mother states matter-of-factly, now aggressively scrubbing a windowsill. "About time. I thought I might die before I got to see the back of them." She pauses. "Even without them there, I won't be able to look at that house and not think of George. Poor, gorgeous boy." You nod absent-mindedly, your stare fixed on your

Doc Martens tapping nervously on the tiled floor.

"I've always wanted to know what happened to him in there," she sighs, shaking her head. "But we know it was evil, whatever it was, so why bother finding out? I'm just thankful that you told me what had gone on – when I went to tell his parents they knew nothing about it! The boy hadn't said a thing!"

"Really?" you ask, flicking your head up. Your fringe slides back to expose your entire face, the jagged cut stretching across your left cheek and the faint black eye to match now fully on display. Your mother's expression transforms from shock to concern to an icy stare.

"What happened to your face?" she demands coldly.

"Nothing, Mum! It happened ages ago – it's practically healed," you add desperately. Your ball your hands into fists, frustrated, scared.

She shrugs, no emotion in her voice or her gestures. "You know, if you didn't dress like a bloody fag, it probably wouldn't have happened."

You recoil in shock. "What did you say?"

"I don't think I need to repeat myself," she replies, almost smugly.

You realise now she might even be enjoying herself, all high and mighty above you, torturing you ever so slowly with her words and her looks and her disdain for all that doesn't quite fit in like she's always done. She's a child holding a magnifying glass over you, an ant, discovering and examining every weakness while watching you burn in shame.

"If you're going to dress and behave like one of them then you have to face the consequences," she continues. "You've brought it on yourse—"

"Don't!" you cry. "Don't say anything more!" Now it's your mother's turn to recoil. You can't remember ever interrupting her.

"How can you say that to me?" You continue furiously. "How can you tell me that other people have the right to beat the shit out of me for minding my own business? For being ga—" Your voice catches in your throat, you gulp, trying to supress the anger, the truth. Put a lid on the cauldron and let the hysteria die down.

But it's too late for that. You have to keep going, have to hurl your self-hatred and frustration right back at her, make her cheeks, her soul, burn with the embarrassment and shame that's been burning inside you for years.

"If you think I deserved to be bashed for looking gay, for being gay Mum, you're evil. You're cruel. You're a witch," you spit, tearing yourself from the kitchen chair and rushing outside with frantic, angry strides. She tries keeping up, but the door slams in her face when you fling it shut behind you.

You hear her calling your name as you storm down the cobbled driveway, gaze fixed on your anxiously awaiting car. As you turn the corner, you see a van pull up just behind it, and then you see Them, arms filled with boxes, smiling at the driver as he turns off the ignition.

It's The Witches. The terrible, fearsome Witches. Weary, grey-haired. A little frail even. It stops you in your tracks. It makes you sad.

Tall Witch turns her long neck and spots you halted beside your car. After a second or two, she smiles, lips pursed, then realises you're shaking, and tears are forming in your eyes.

"Hello, Katie," she says gently. "Are you alright?"

You force out a jolted laugh, biting your lip to stop yourself from crying. "I'm always all right."

"It's nice to see you," she adds after a painfully long pause. "I suppose this could be the last time Miriam and I talk to you if you don't come back and visit soon – our last day here is next week, you see. We're going to a retireme—"

"What happened that day with George Michaels?" you blurt. Your mouth has become unregulated by your brain – everything is so disjointed.

Tall Witch stops, stares, takes a long, deep breath. "I thought you knew. You told your mother a whole story, after all."

You inhale sharply, shaking your head. "No, what really happened?" you ask, as gently as possible.

She turns her head away momentarily, before locking her deep brown, weary eyes onto yours. "He caught us in bed together," she sighs. "He had snuck in through an open window and was trying to steal the wooden carving in the room next to our bedroom, the one you could see from the front of the house." You nod, remembering the exact carving.

"We were so petrified people would find out," she adds. "It was illegal then."

"I'm sorry," you whisper finally, voice and body tense. "I'm sorry I believed you were villains – told people you were."

Tall Witch shrugs. "You weren't the only one that did."

You both stand awkwardly, until you add: "I've never even known your name."

Her eyes light up, happy and sad all at once. "It's Kathleen."

A Strange Affection

Christopher Marcatili

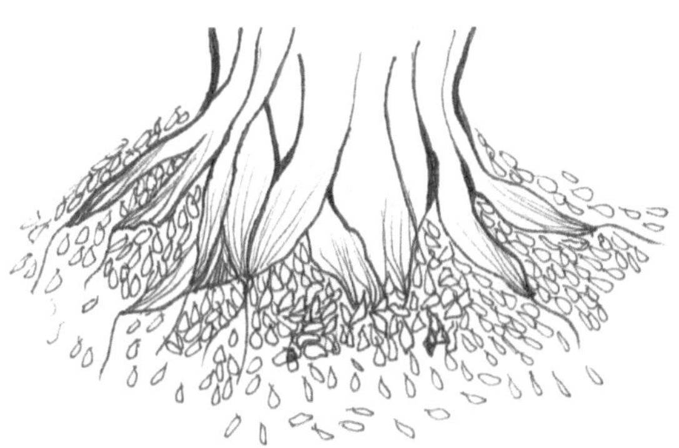

Jaime and I sit beneath one of the Moreton Bay figs where, years ago now, we met face to face. An awkward meeting, even as first dates go. Him arriving fifteen minutes late, no message or warning. Out of breath, having run from the station, yet somehow still smiling, still charming. For the first five minutes he could barely speak, made no apology. Me over-dressed compared, shirt pressed, wearing a ring I got for my eighteenth.

Now roots of the Moreton Bays enfold us, embrace us, force us close together. Their fruits, half-eaten and strewn on the grass of the Botanical Gardens make for an uncomfortable bed, but neither of us complain. The day is too beautiful. Now we sit with a bottle of red, store-bought figs, blue cheese for me and brie for him. Nearby, the lady's chair a great uncomfortable slab overlooking the harbour.

That first meeting, as we walk the gardens, night has already fallen. Jaime explains he brought something for us to eat, that we needed no restaurant. In the darkness, I don't see but rather sense the cheeky grin on his face and then he shows me what he's brought: a box of children's cereal, two plastic cups swiped from a convenience store Slushy dispenser, and a small carton of milk.

I frown. 'No spoon?'

But we don't need spoons, he tells me. Not when we have cups.

Later, after the milky mess of our dinner, he climbs one of the trees. More graceful than I, who remain on the grass looking up after a failed attempt to climb. It has often been that way between us; Jaime goes where I dare not, but sometimes he manages to bring me along behind him.

The night ends as awkwardly as it began, with a hug and a kiss that lands somewhere between lips and cheek. The promise to see each other again, but only half-made.

In the morning, I realise I've lost my ring. Not valuable, but beloved all the same. I message Jaime but he says he doesn't remember seeing it. The loss of the ring is the perfect annoying end to a night that I already look back on half embarrassed, half with a strange affection.

The day brings work, a humdrum occupation in the city, where I find myself wondering why I didn't try harder to climb the tree, why I didn't laugh at the cereal and cups instead of frown.

I return to the Gardens after work. In the late afternoon the trees shine with a halo of light, the harbour shimmers. I know I won't find the ring, but I need to look. Surprise on my face when I see him, kneeling in the grass, embraced by the swan-necked Moreton Bay roots, looking for it too.

Killing for Love

Brooke Forbes

I wonder how many people have killed for love. Pure love. Love that propels you. Love that starts with a heart tick and ends in a tug of pain. The type that rips at your skin and frees you—if only momentarily—from the spinning cage.

I've thought about people in the same situation as me; a man in a jealous rage, a woman protecting her young, a wife escaping a long battle. I've thought about how righteousness and justice worked in or against their favour. I've thought about long battles and short battles, apologetic releases and victory celebrations; the wrongly convicted and criminals locked away.

Away is where I currently am. It's not a place, it's more of a space. Time here is irrelevant and thoughts span across unmarked days. I'm in the limbo of a cell, between an act and a judgement, between a life and a life lost. I can feel the people before me; their crimes, their lack of crimes, their voices, their thoughts, layered into the pores of the concrete, oozing from the air like mould spores. It's a build-up that carries the weight of history. And I'm in the middle of it, sitting still, silently breathing in the toxicity.

What difference does it make to collect their stories, I wonder? Should I try to piece them together, like a long, reverberating tapestry?

No amount of precedent and past lives can help me through this process. I know why I'm here: I am here because I loved. I am here because I killed.

***

Audrey walked directly into Melia on the way out of Pink Salt, turning suddenly, stumping her toe on the corner of the bar.

"Rough night?" Melia said, suppressing a laugh. Audrey smiled and stepped to the left, knowing she couldn't hold her stare for too long, feeling the eyes of at least three men on her back.

Audrey had seen Melia around Plymouth – wearing a check shirt and faded jeans at H&M, flicking through magazines at a local Newsagent and sitting in the middle of a roundabout with a group of bar tenders, laughing and finishing a shared pizza. There was something about her that made Audrey want to piece Melia's story together – where was she going, who was she socialising with, where did she work and how could Audrey get to know her better.

Their meeting wasn't an accident. Audrey had finished an extended Friday night at Stephens and Scown, a corporate law firm in the Barbican, refusing an invitation for dinner with colleagues and instead choosing to place herself in Melia's path. Each time Audrey ran into Melia she noticed her hair first, bright blonde and mid-length, and then her eyes, dark and azure purple. She noticed her boyish mannerisms, and a laugh that cut through noise. But always present was a familiar barrier – stares from a male bar tender, stares from an ex-boyfriend, stares from a boss. She'd been through this trying to date before, she knew the rules. It was a barrier that said you're not welcome here, entry not allowed.

Audrey knew Pink Salt was key in breaking down the barrier. Their first conversations had to happen there, somewhere at the back of the bar, below the neon signs, next to the DJ or in the smoking area outside. At the time Pink Salt was a corner faux dive bar in the backstreets of Plymouth, housing a combination of student underground and wandering travellers. It had been through a quick succession of recent ownership – Porters, a whisky bar filled with drunken, back-slapping navy men and Stacy's, an up-market strip club that attracted a similar clientele. The stripper signs still hung there, glowing an eerie green.

It was the sixth time Audrey ran into Melia at Pink Salt that she almost went in for a kiss. "Back again?" Melia said, knowing they'd meet each other's acquaintance.

"Like clockwork." Audrey said, regretting every syllable.

Somewhere between a Melon Ball and a Silver Bullet Audrey nearly leant in, asking Melia to hold a lull in conversation, thinking of tucking Melia's hair behind her ear. It was the type of feigned moment Audrey was hyper-sensitive to – not here, her better instincts overrode, it's not quite safe right here.

Audrey and Melia's meetings at Pink Salt steadily grew in intensity, both hoping to graduate from light conversation to a first date, or maybe even a first kiss, somewhere in the alley smoking area, away from any watching eyes.

Melia wasn't the first girl Audrey had courted, but she knew too well what it was like to be courted herself. She thought about how men had watched her younger self, interrupted her and tricked her into kissing them. She knew the feeling of being stalked and wanted. There was a sense of power in flipping these dynamics, in being the hunter rather than the hunted.

The turning point was Saturday night after Melia's best friend's hens do. At around 10:30pm Melia burst through the door of Pink Salt with a huge amount of laughter and three female friends at her arms, all of them in burlesque, all looking like a Victoria Secret model meets vampire grunge. Audrey could barely look at Melia. Her entire body was wrapped in painted permanent ink Japanese blossoms with branches dipping down her arms and across her chest. Over the body art, she wore a cut-out jumpsuit with a tight, gemmed bodice, holding her smallish breasts as high as possible. She topped the look off with some fake vampire fangs and the darkest smoky eyes Audrey had ever seen. This is going to be the night, Audrey thought, quickly stepping back and avoiding eye contact. I'll ask her out tonight.

When Audrey sees Melia she tucks herself into the smoking alley, needing a moment to gather strength. Melia enters the room, locking eyes with Audrey quickly, smiling and walking across to meet her, a Scandinavian cider in hand. She's tipsy, Audrey thought, this could be dangerous. Melia hugs Audrey, but this time she runs her hand down her lower back, pulling herself back slightly. Audrey can see where the ink on her skin has bled, she can feel the softness of her breath. Not here, Audrey keeps thinking, struggling to maintain any sense of self, we aren't quite safe here.

What followed was a quick succession of events – Audrey feels a violent crack, the air splits, Melia's face distorts and Audrey can only remember Melia's Japanese skin art altered with the finest spray of blood.

***

The events before the killing of Luke Porter are etched into my mind in cold fragments. It's recorded in tiny sentences, strung together with long, nauseating pauses. Every time I read them it becomes something more and more obscure, more and more disconnected from me – it's something that happened to another person, at another place, a long time ago.

Here are some of the details, one more time, for you all to review:

Audrey, 27, leaves Stephens and Scown on the 19th August 2020. She's wearing a blue pencil skirt and white shirt. She enters Pink Salt at 8:30pm.

Melia, 24, arrives at Pink Salt at 10:35pm, wearing a vampire burlesque outfit.

Audrey and Melia run into each other in the smoking section.

Melia leans into Audrey.

Luke Porter lunges at Audrey from behind.
A fight ensues.

In my mind now I refer to it as the kill. It's not a murder, it's not an accident, it's not entirely self-defence. I haven't been able to remember in exact detail how the kill happened. I've been told Melia leant in for a kiss, that Luke Porter stalked Melia to the bar in the first place and that he saw red at Melia daring to nearly kiss me. I know Luke was holding a knife. I know Melia swung at Luke. I know the knife dropped to the ground before I picked it up.

But there's also a softness that lingers when I think of the kill. It's the type of a softness that melts through a scene like falling snow. And when it melts my senses fall into a void, if only momentarily, eventually fading into a slow and satisfying release.

***

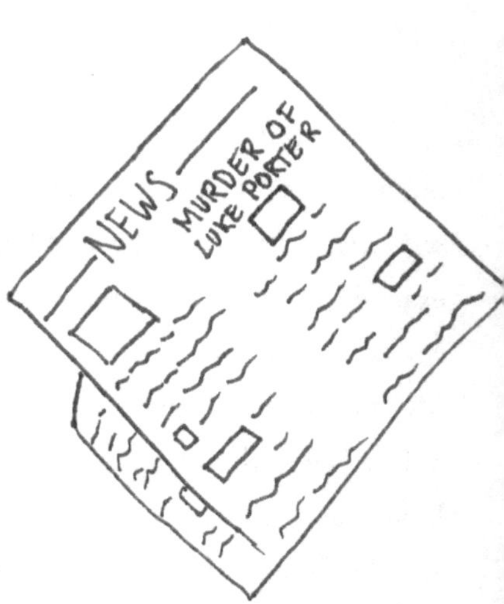

Souvenir

Anthony Markel

He sat down beside me. We smiled sweetly at each other and he greeted me with a nod, his arms clasped casually between his legs.

"Hey."

"Hello," I said in reply, my hands awkwardly tucked under my thighs.

I tried not to look at him too much for the sake of his comfort, but his face was intoxicating. It had changed a little though, and now he had an attempt at a beard and a piercing in one ear. I ventured a little at these changes with darting glances and was privately amused at what might have inspired these adventurous decisions. I was suddenly reminded of what other changes in his life may have occurred and nervously looked down at his hands, but they had no ring. I breathed a sigh of relief. The shakes had returned to me now that I was in his presence again, and along with it a cold sweat. I tried to still myself.

An awkward silence prevailed for a few moments. I could see there was some strain in his face, he frowned and stared at the ground.

"Hey man," he choked a little on his words as he broke the ice "I'm sorry about what happened."

I contemplated his words, feeling emotions rise and swell.

"I'm sorry too." I decided was the best response. It was well meant.

We looked into each other in the eyes with a little surprise and sympathy. But the moment fell as we succumbed to guilt. We both wanted to tell each other that it wasn't the other's fault, but that lie had lost its luster and now we accepted the bitter truth that we both still bore resentment for what the other had done. Everything was understood in those few words that planted the hard truth in front of us like an obstinate metal box.

I breathed, and my anxiety eased a little. My courage to be myself in front of him and speak plainly what I felt awoke and filled my body with confidence and normality. I found a memory floating in the darkness of my mind giving a fluttering illumination to a vast chasm of hollow thought.

"Do you remember," I began, my eyes turned up to the warm blue sky. "Do you remember when I asked you out?" A playful smile came across my lips and was reciprocated by a fond chuckle from him.

"Yeah, I remember."

"I remember I told some stupid story about how classical music was connected to modern music because of a lyric I heard somewhere. It sounded so much better in my mind but as soon as it came out I felt insane!" I smiled with my teeth and let nostalgia smooth over the roughness of the past.

"I gotta admit, I was a bit confused." I was happy then because he talked earnestly and playfully, like he would talk to friend.

The sun was warm on us both.

"And of course, you said, 'why not' and that was the dream come true. And then we sat there for the rest of lunch not saying a word. It was like we were both in shock trying to understand what had just happened and what we were really going to do, you know?" I said.

"But, I didn't really know it was a date though. I just thought you wanted to go out as friends," he replied, the clarification bearing some sting.

"No, no, I know that. I remember I knew it because after you agreed I was still unsatisfied. Because, I suppose it hadn't turned out the way

I planned." I chose my words delicately to hide my emotion.

He looked at me with an unexpectant curiosity, his eyebrows raised, anticipating me opening up about my thoughts and feelings from that day. I remembered that look with fondness for days gone by and bitterness for his treatment to me.

I continued.

"I suppose I looked rather foolish, or strange."

He said nothing.

"I could tell, you know, that you didn't really want to go with me. You were just doing the right thing, like when your mother tells you to invite the kid with no friends over to your house." A slow bitterness from my words seeped into the air and turned it hard. He was frowning at the ground again now. We had lost both our smiles.

"And then, I remember, there was that girl who would sit with you every now and then. She walked past." I could see this peaked his curiosity and he looked back up at me, with a little bit of concern for what I would say next. I spoke more slowly now.

"Yes, she saw me, and she saw you and she saw the connection. I remember the look she gave you as she walked past, it was a kind of sweet empathy, because, you see, you were giving up your lunchtime to sit with the lonely, sad boy who was probably a little crazy." My words had dropped their filter now and were passive aggressive as I retold the story from what I understood was the girls point of view.

He could not deny that my words held truth to them, and I saw the guilt on his face. My suspicions that he'd had feelings for this girl whom I knew nothing about pierced my heart with malicious pins as they were confirmed by his expressions. I could see he was struggling with what I said and was trying to justify his actions in his mind. Anger was there on his face that he had been unjustly accused.

The sun had gone behind a cloud now, and the cold penetrated our bodies like sad music. We both knew we were alone.

"But never mind that, you've said you're sorry" I made an effort to smile and patch things up, but the wound I opened up had gushed forth too much pain to be swept aside so easily. Now my face was full and heavy.

I realised that we had not forgiven each other yet, and I contemplated whether those words would hold any truth to them. There hadn't been a day where I wasn't ready to beg to God to give me another chance to talk to him, that things might be resolved. Now that chance was here, though it felt empty and indifferent. I wanted to forgive him and make everything better, but my emotions held me back.

He spoke, and I was liberated from the prison of my thoughts.

"Mate, I.." He choked on his words again. "I… I care about you."

He stopped awkwardly, but his message could not have been clearer. I could feel a sharpness in my throat as I stared at him, sitting ashamedly with his head in his palm. I felt his words deeply and understood them completely. It was a strange friendship that we shared, but it was real.

"I know," I said, merely a whisper.

We could not look into each other's eyes in that moment for fear that we may lose control of our emotions. We could not touch each other because we did not know each other that well and we were both men. But we felt what the other felt, and the cold went away.

A car rolled up to side walk and the time for him to go had come. We both stood up, looked each other in the eye and said goodbye, and he got in the car and it drove away. I watched without blinking that I might take in every last moment, until the car went around a bend and he disappeared.

When we decided that we would meet I was worried that it would just become another memory, but he had given me something more than a memory. I knew the feeling would stay with me always.

Immersed in liquid silver

Jenny Blackford

All she wanted was one last hour alone, in the pool at the river's bend, before she died.

Drowning was not an easy path to Persephone's eternal realm, but the marriage that Melia's father the king had arranged for her would certainly have been a harsher one. Slaves talked to servants, underlings to traders, soldiers to captured warriors across kingdoms and borders. If only half the rumours brought to

Melia were true, the distant prince her father had chosen for her would be her death.

The prince's first wife had fallen from a cliff, after her singing failed to please her new husband. His next wife had collapsed and died at a banquet a month after she'd produced a second daughter, not the required son.

Despite this, Melia's father accepted the distant prince's offer for her hand, the culmination of a years-long auction of influence, diplomacy and wealth. Melia was sound breeding stock, her father a powerful ruler. A fine bride-price of lapis lazuli, golden cups and strong bronze swords, sent by the prince, now lined Melia's father's treasury.

"It's your duty, girl," the king said. "Your children will be the meat and blood of the alliance between our kingdoms. This marriage is what princesses like you are for."

Now the day was almost here. The expedition would leave at dawn, taking Melia over the mountain pass and across two rivers to her future husband. The palace buzzed with preparations. Horses were groomed, soldiers equipped, and wagons packed with embroidered gowns, cloaks, shoes, and silver-inlaid furniture for her boudoir. Almost alone, the cause of the fuss but far from the centre of the work, Melia planned her escape.

For the first time since she broke a precious bowl at four years old, she lied to her old nurse. "I need my beauty sleep. I mustn't disappoint my husband, when he sees me. What would my father say?" Melia did not add, I've always disappointed him.

Nurse would not miss Melia, not too much. After years of tending a mere princess, she had a healthy baby prince to spend her days and nights fretting over. The king's new wife (a sweet-natured royal girl only a few years older than Melia) had done her duty in just ten months, produced a sturdy boy – as Melia must, if she submitted to her destiny.

Instead, she ran away.

\#

The palace guards, with their boars-tusk helmets almost covering their eyes, were easy for the princess to deceive. They would have done anything for one of Melia's smiles.

"I go this evening to lay a flower on my mother's grave for the last time," she said, trying to hide the strain of deception in her voice. She stood straight as one of the men's bronze spears, as a princess ought. "My five slaves must come with me. She knew them all. Your captain will keep us safe."

She smiled widely, and the guards' eyes melted. She would miss them far more than she'd miss her father.

\#

After they had offered flowers on her mother's grave – that much of what the princess told the guards was true – Melia sent her five female slaves far from the harsh palace, with the captain of the guard as guide. They wouldn't lack in their new lives; through the last month, Melia had sewn gems and gold into the seams of their new clothes.

"One last adventure," the captain said. "I'll take good care of them. I'll take them home, every one of them, away from here. They are free people now." He grinned and turned away, trying to hide his tears.

His loyalty to Melia was stronger than his vows to the king; he had no cause to stay. His wife had died of fever in a winter storm two years ago, with their three sons already lost in the king's endless foreign wars, their daughter dead in childbed, and the baby too.

A last embrace for all, and they were gone into the night.

Father would be angry, but it didn't matter. He couldn't hurt Melia now. She had nowhere to go but to her death. One last hour, alone, in the pool at the river's bend, was all she asked.

\#

The waterlilies were luminous as ghosts in the moonlight. What were those pale shapes that moved beneath the lilies, far too big for fish, seaweed-green hair trailing to the river bed, arms waving slowly in the water, slim feet treading water? Nurse had warned her of water nymphs, more beautiful and dangerous than white wolves on the mountain. The princess looked again; saw nothing but the lilies, and the pool.

Melia floated, immersed in liquid silver. Her toes, her fingers, hair, everything was coated thick with it.

Soon icy currents flowed around her arms and legs – and, as she sank, a naiad's liquid tongue was in her mouth, sweet and arousing and lovely. Their mouths melted together. If this was death, it was far more alluring than she'd been led to expect.

\#

Melia slept that night in Rhoe's watery arms, wrapped by the naiad's seaweed hair, and woke surprised and then delighted to be alive, and loved.

They slept and woke and ate and loved, and slept again. The king's soldiers tramped the hills, but who would dare to search the naiads' pool by moonlight?

When the moon waxed, and waned, and waxed again, the princess and the water nymphs celebrated her un-wedding. Rhoe's sisters brought the princess and her love, floating in the pool, dishes of duck eggs piled with shaded cress, poached brown trout with melted sorrel sauce, frogs' legs in ponds of aspic like wobbly water, and sweet-fleshed crays from muddy river banks.

Melia washed the dishes afterwards. Nurse had taught her well.

Months trickled past, all languid afternoons and starlit nights of love.

#

The old captain of the guard sat high on the edge of the pool, keeping a discreet distance.

"Your former slaves are home, my Princess. Two of them in Babylon, and one each in Syria, Egypt, Thrace. All are safe now, back with the families the slavers stole them from. Along the way I saw places I never thought I would, and heard no good anywhere of the prince your father chose to be your husband."

The princess nodded.

He frowned. "But you, here, now, under the sky, naked with the water-nymphs, almost one of them. A compromising position for a princess. Your mother would . . ."

Trembling. "Yes?"

A flash of teeth, white in the moonlight.

His voice breaking, just a little. "I brought her often to this pool when she was big with you, and later, after you were born. You crawled here on the grass, floated in the pool held in her arms.

She would rejoice that you are here, that you are loved."

"Truly? My mother?" the princess asked, tears in her eyes.

"Truly. I brought her here whenever she could leave the palace without risk. Now and then the naiads showed themselves to her. It is an honour for any mortal to see them, as I tonight am honoured." He bowed his head.

Tears dripped Melia's cheeks. "But why has no one told me this?"

Rhoe flowed at her right side. "Your father distrusts everyone and everything. Your mother was afraid that you might suffer if any others knew she came here, swam in our pool, and sometimes saw us. Even you, when you were young, might blurt it unawares. Once you could speak, her visits ceased. But we remember her with love."

Rhoe wiped Melia's tears with water-silvered hands, and kissed her damply till she smiled again.

#

Trout rainbowed the pool; naiads lifted seven shining fish up onto the clean grass of the river bank. The captain cleaned them, built a fire, found wild thyme to stuff them with. River-water turned to bubbling wine as it sparkled into mouths and throats. They feasted together through the night, slept through the day, then rejoiced again.

The captain's palace life was finished forever, and his last adventure done. He built a forest hut a short walk from the river pool, and visited at night with furred or feathered treats to share with them, happier than he'd been since his wife and children were all alive.

#

Naiads are near-immortal, and Melia lived close enough to them for their longevity to flow through her. She saw the captain age and die, and grieved for him more than for her father. Her half-brother was a kinder king than their shared parent, and the land prospered.

Princess Melia ate many banquets through her long, strange watery life. But in the end, she looped back time and again to the feast at the captain's return, as the river looped around the bend.

LOW PRICES!
500
PROFESSO
SLEEP

The Darlinghurst Discount

Erin Riley

We weren't in Darlinghurst when we got the Darlinghurst Discount. We were deep in Sydney's factory-outlet promised land, Alexandria, at the homemaker centre. Buying a bed.

If someone had told me that one day, I would be buying a bed at a homemaker centre, looking into my future's bright blue eyes, in the middle of Captain Snooze, as the electronic mattress profiler whirred into gear, lowered by a charismatic queer man called Barry, I'd have said fuck right off.

In the past, I had never been able to see what was ahead, to make plans for the future – my relationships, the romantic ones at least, felt often so precarious. Like the idea of planning a family, buying a bed with someone else, indicated an investment in each other. In the hope of a shared future. It communicated a sense of certainty, a willingness to stick around.

You, at thirty-seven, had never bought a new bed. Always collected from the side of the road, discarded or forwarded on by upwardly mobile friends. Too much of an investment for someone who had moved around so much and never planned to settle down. Who, like me, believed that every relationship would end and went into new relationships with the hope of enjoying things while they lasted. Forever until it wasn't any fun anymore. My mantra, more macabre than yours, Forever Until It's Shit, saw me languishing in relationships that had long lost their shine.

But you had landed back in Sydney and after floating on the periphery of one another's lives for over a decade we found in each other a certainty never known.

*

We were buying our new bed with money from our parents. Yours had bought your brothers' beds as wedding gifts. This extravagance, something you never believed would be extended to you. Though, so much had shifted in the time between then and my meeting you.

And so, we found ourselves at the homemaker centre one wintry weekend mid-afternoon to find our bed. After jumping all over a few beds in one store, we darted off to another to compare. Both anxious people, we liked the idea of trialling beds and working out what it was that we wanted on our own. Being swamped by sales people felt overwhelming.

But then we met Barry. Barry with his bulbous belly, his navy woollen vest with its V Neck over a short-sleeved button up. Barry with his tiny, devious, all-knowing sultana eyes. His effeminate, familiar charm, his deeply comforting queerness. Barry spotted us - two anxious queers trying to feel their way in the bed shop – another space, like the world, not quite made for the comfort of people like us.

We folded softly into Barry's reassuring and knowledgeable hands as he, despite my darkened moustachioed upper lip, gave us 'girls' the royal treatment.

'Are you side or tummy sleepers?' Barry quizzed us.

'I'm often referred to as a beautiful log', I say, craning my neck in your direction, referencing your apt description of my default tummy sleep positioning.

'I can imagine.' He flirted back.

We told him you liked to mix it up – a versatile sleeper.

We knew we were after a firm to hard mattress and so after our futuristic turn on the mattress-depth-charger we were both shocked to hear we were being recommended SOFT.

'NO!', we cried out collectively. Barry reassured us that our incompatible sleep positions was reason enough for this recommendation – a matressy middle ground.

Barry asked us about our budget. What we wanted. Ideally we'd spend it all on a mattress and deal with the bed frame like most other items we needed; by shouting loudly into the Internet, offering to trade our quick pickles for a soon-to-be-tossed unwanted bed frame. Having this much money to play with, especially for you of the perennial free bed, meant the decision carried with it so much weight. Are you sure?' you said to me, lazing on the FIRM Slumberland, me, struggling not to be swallowed by the SOFT

Sealy Posturepedic, 'it's so much money, we have to be SURE.'

I couldn't help but laugh. You had been sleeping, and me too since we met, much like the princess and the pea, on an uncomfortably lumpy situation that was rescued from a curb-side collection. Everything we had perched on was infinitely more comfortable.

*

Barry sometimes spoke in the third person which was oddly comforting. He looked a bit like a gay Alec Baldwin.

'Don't worry, Barry's going to look after you. I'm going to give you the Darlinghurst Discount!'

There is something deeply pleasurable in being seen and read as queer by those of the same ilk.

The subtle references, the furtive nods on the street, an acknowledgement of shared otherness. Barry didn't need to say any more than that, his Darlinghurst Discount screamed 'I see you, I'm an absolute freak too! We must look after each other!' And, so we lapped up our momentary gay privilege.

We engaged in theatrical recreations of our own night-life on the many mattresses. I flung myself onto the bed, face down, perched stiff as a board, you with your butt softly resting against my leg. Your face, turned away from mine. We acted out all our pre-sleeping permutations – you spooning me, your hand laid over the small of my back, the puzzle-like embrace, tummy to tummy, legs intertwined, my arm under your neck, holding you in a bear-hug, me trying to be a better side sleeper and spooning you only to dip back onto my belly, my right hand, blindly reaching for your left, where we so often fell asleep – hand in hand.

In between our bedroom calisthenics, Barry perched on the edge of a nearby bed and we talked about sleep. I had just finished a book on the science of sleep and was now determined to give myself an eight-hour sleep window after discovering that sleep debt can never be repaid. Barry got ten hours of sleep a night. Barry got ten hours of sleep a night. He told us the benefits of the $200 mattress protector that he would be giving us for free. 'It's great for if you enjoy drinking wine in bed' he said. I wondered about Barry's sleep hygiene and considered lending him my book.

We spoke about the pros and cons of ensemble base vs bed frame. Barry preferred ensembles. He didn't even have a 'skirt' for his. He had just repurposed a black double fitted sheet.

'How important is easy-access to three sides of the bed for you?' Barry asked.

'Vital!' came our enthusiastic reply.

God he was good. I looked at you and your bright blue eyes smiled back at me.

I had long held shame about being queer and kept partners at arms-length from my family. Though, years of therapy had dislodged the shame and the more I liked myself, the more my outsider status was intolerable. I found compassion for them and understood the ways in which socialised norms had infected them with dangerous myths. Myths that families either replicate or reject. Queers who fitted into mainstream cultural imaginings of gender and sexuality were tolerable for them, but me, with my rough edges, left them in a sort of existential parental distress. And so, our parents' collective bed-buying, symbolically, meant a lot. Their investment, quite literally, in our gay sex, the ultimate act of contrition.

And so, with our Darlinghurst Discount, we left the homemaker centre with a renewed faith in family. Barry, himself, a simple reminder that capitalism fucks us all, especially those living more marginal lives like queers– often more precariously employed, less privileged. Barry didn't know us, but his willingness to carve into inflated prices for two queer freaks, a benevolent reminder that queer family runs deep, with ready access to all sides of the bed.

Before He Gets To Your Door

Quinn Eades

In the brief flicker between Melbourne lock downs, June 2020, a man who had been messaging me for months on a dating app asked if he could come over. I was unsure about him. His lack of a profile picture, which meant on this app he appeared as a ghost floating inside a black square, disturbed me. The sparse information in his actual profile bothered me. A muffled fright pushed up into my throat when I got his message, almost could not be stifled but it was.

Think now of a life being trained to ignore my own instincts, to downplay, to dismiss, to submit and to fawn. To be sweet and willing and eager to please as my prime means of survival. Think now *listen, listen to that stifled alarm, that body shiver, see the danger signs please please now before he even gets to your door my love see the signs.*

That night he messaged me insistently with dick pics and *invite me overs.* When I said I was feeling tired and vulnerable after just moving house his response was, again, *invite me over.* After an hour or so, tired, ignoring the signs, mildly curious, trying to explore I said *ok.* I said *ok let's have a cider and talk about what we might like to do together* which to me seemed clear, which to me seemed as if I had said *you coming here to my home is not sex it is talking and sharing a drink,* and forty five minutes later he was at my front door.

Think now of the psychology paper I read recently on a neurological phenomenon known as 'The Doorway Effect', where studies show that a person's ability to remember is significantly impacted by walking through a doorway. Think now of this door, of the door I let him through, of leading him from there through double glass sliding doors to my lounge room, of what warnings rang out and then were forgotten in the place between, in the *through* and *in* and *having been* and *will be*. Imagine a life lived in the *not yet*, in the verge.

When I opened my front door there he was, bulky, chin bristling and rough, 6 pack under his arm, thick dirty white coloured woollen jumper, jeans, boots, blue baseball cap with an Australian flag on the front. Again that feeling of being troubled, bothered, disturbed... and then the sickening slip that comes from muffling and dismissing, repeatedly, every internal alarm system I have that says *run, it is about to happen again, get out, fight, shut the door in his face, run, it is about to happen again.*

I think now of marching before I could walk, of being raised by feminist lesbian ratbags in the seventies and eighties who made sure we knew we lived and grew on stolen Gadigal Land, of painting a huge Aboriginal flag at aftercare with my sister for the Land Rights march the next day, the staff bemused and looking on. I think now that I am yet to meet a patriot I trust or like, feel the slip slipping again, where slip is the slurry of clay and also the moment that triggers the fall. Feel my terror muffled because *don't be judgemental, he could be a nice person, look he's come all this way to your door with cider he even asked you what kind you liked when he stopped at the bottle-o, because...*

I let him in.

He left an hour and a half a year a cycling century a horror movie later. He left but not before he had walked around my house and told me it was a *very big place for someone who lived alone*, not before he sat on my couch, clothes now on, legs spread, and told me how boring his life was. I was polite while he did this. Agreeable. Friendly even. I perched as far from him as I could while he drank his cider. Kept smiling but finally was able, in a pause between his recited miseries, to say *I was tired* and *might need some time to be alone now*.

He walked out of my front door and I locked the screen door (I had never locked it before) as soon as it was closed but he didn't leave. He's still here, but not in doorways. He's still here, in my house. He is behind me if my back is not against a wall.

My neck bristles and my throat hurts and I try to stay in the frame in the door out of the way but he is in every navy blue sheet I threw out the next day.

He is in the bed I dismantled and put into my shed the next day, the mattress he had flipped and turned and turned me to stone on.

He is in the shadow shifted space between front window and camelia tree at the front of my house when it is night.

He is in the pivot of muscle and bone that is my jaw. One year later it is still hard to eat anything that requires extended chewing and I find myself still living on cereal and tea and yoghurt and soft fruit.

He is at my back door, looking up at the silver lock, he is inside me, over me, through me.

He is around my neck, his hands pushed down (it's my fault I told him in one message how much I *liked it rough*) hard and fast my breath momentarily gone he was sitting astride me, he pulled his hands away and turned his hands to fists and then made a face that said *you are lucky I stopped doing that*, dropped his arms, turned me around, kept going.

I could not get the smell of him off me for days for weeks for months. I felt strongly that he had stolen my face (he had stolen my face). I stopped being able to stand in the shower. I sat (I still do) in the cold tile corner, water hitting the top of my scalp and then running down the sound drowning tinnitus not drowning a voice that says over and over you are gone. I sat as long as it stayed hot. Tore my heat softened toenails off one by one by one without flinching. Scrubbed my face my neck kept my eyes closed.

And now this. Now this vital (again) public conversation about gender-based violence. White cis male politicians no longer able to get away with their excruciating and nonsensical 'these women are our mothers and daughters and sisters' revelations in the face of yet another disclosure, yet another woman who carries the burden of proof.

I carry the burden of proof too. I carry the reply to my police statement, which said there would be no investigation because 'there is nothing in your words to indicate that he knew what he was doing was non-consensual'.

I carry the knowledge I have now, about straight men trawling for trans men and trans masc people on gay dating apps, that these men use our vulnerabilities and transness against us to get and to take exactly what they want.

I carry the many and devastating stories of gender-based violence my trans and gender diverse family, friends, lovers and others have both survived and not survived.

I carry my trans queer histories, I attend to creativity and connection and joy, I attend to pleasure and intensities and love, the way LGBTQIA+ communities have been doing for longer than we can ever know.

And now I carry a call and speak from the doorway the edge the ledge. A call to remember all of us who bear the load of white toxic masculinity and have lost or are losing our lives because we do not have the body or the gender or the sexuality that our attacker thinks we should have. To include trans and gender diverse people when discussing gender-based violence. Every time. No exceptions. Please.

Love Sick, 20
Bio:

Love Sick

Jack Bastock

1.

It is spring and my Grindr bio is as follows: "Don't be pushy. Not into rough. Not into dom." My pic is a gritty, forward-camera selfie through a shitty mirror in my room. A slim smooth shirtless boy in short shorts, books and speakers fringing the mantlepiece. What was it that did it for him? How I said I liked to fuck? How I looked as pixels? Or did I just get lucky, first to msg a "Fresh Face" on the banner of the meat grind? What did he like / what did he like / what did he like / in me?

2.

I was turning over the scene of our date; of stroking the small of his back; of brushing my fingers in his hands; of fingering the hair on his arms; of him saying I could stay the night … if I wanted.

I was thinking of our date; of how he texted late, and how this made it a booty call, and how had it come to this? Of how his friends asked me nothing and how they seemed to know something I didn't?

Of how he told me his friends' dirty little secrets; of how it still did not feel like fucking so much as making; of how in his room cheap love songs I would have skipped seemed, somehow, to be miraculous.

3.

We met when my work also felt fraudulent. He asked *what are you up to*. I said *I'm doing writing*. He said *good luck*, but in the tone of giving distinctly few fucks (echoing the world in which my work was not getting picked up).

Later, he asked what I was writing. I said: I'm trying something new. I said: songs of broken hearts. He said cool, but his voice was all the more hollow. He did not know, of course, that they were already about him.

4.

Nor did he know they weren't songs, really, but spoken word poems I pictured reading at open mics with jazz backings à la Wanda Robinson, whose smokey, heart-hurting records *Black Ivory* (1971) and *Me and a Friend* (1973) I had on repeat, having found in them the only timbre that matched with how I hurt.

5.

September. I could have sworn I saw him at a café on Albion & Bartow, where I was riding a caffeine high, telling a friend all about him at a table in the sun. I thought: he's too tall to be you. But then that same jaw, that same rocking roll gait, that same curly, Greek bust hair. I looked right at him, but he walked right on. When I saw him next, he said he didn't remember. But oh oh,

I am sure of it now. For of course he'd walk right by me. Omen. Synecdoche.

6.

Among the advice that has never made sense to me: "just be yourself". Cool, which one? My spirit animal being the Other, I shift my shape to match where I am, who I'm with, what I'm doing, what I'm saying, etc. I chose, by and large, to show the sides of me most like him (or how he presented): friendly, easy, low-key, a mystery. There was more to us both; but it had no occasion to play out. There was none of the post-nap me, the me with friend x, the moi with friend y, the krunk destructor, the chatty Jack in low-light, the chilled cat at twilight, the jacked-up Jack home from a night out. But now, of course, there is nothing more brain-disturbing than how he might have felt about *them*.

*

How, for instance, I made him search and search and search for the song I'd heard as we snoozed post-coitus. No, not that one. No. Next.

Can't be that. Ad nauseum. (Never one to hide my 'weird'—but whence the notion that it is endearing? I'm not so much playing @ eccentric, with a lil insecurity that it is 'annoying'; nor am I convinced of being any more interesting, or any less dysfunctional. It is just this: that I will hide no part of me. None. "Are not excess and madness my truth, my strength?" (Barthes, *A Lover's Discourse*).

*

Still, the fear knocks at the memory: if only I'd been more 'normal' (predictable?), more varsity gay, more white collared-shirt with chino shorts, more *straight*forward. If only he'd seen a different side, or I'd been someone else at that moment.

*

Then, as now, the song I'd heard in bed was a sort of assurance. Words of the kind I could not get from him. Naturally, I want to quote it here, together with all the other love fluff, but my lips are sealed by copyright law. There is only the title to quote, as if assigning some required listening: *Two Brothers*, Hanni El Khatib. Album: Moonlight.

7.

Summer. I send a 1,000 word text, complete with paragraphs and a concluding statement (like I said: love sick). In summary:

-If it was just sex why the fuck did you ....

    -want to hang out

    -invite me out to gigs

    -introduce me to your friends

-There's chemistry

    -Did you notice

-Yeah, I have 'feelings'

    -But I always did

    -You knew

    -And it didn't stop you before

-Friends with benefits is in no way 'serious'

8.

Witness the mind in pieces. Everything is suspect: neither good nor bad, true nor false. /

He couldn't stay over cause he had work early, or a "dentist appointment" or "stuff to do" (or cause we'd blown and were done?). He asked me to the party so he could see me (or cause there was no one there as fuckable?). They are not so much memories as material. Fodder for a hermeneutic fractal. "Everything signifies" and so "I entrap myself, I bind myself in calculations, I keep myself from enjoyment" (Barthes).

*

As, for example, when he came inside me when I'd told him not to. For months I'd laughed-off bareback. "But, you know, with certain people," he said, a sentiment that he apparently extended to jizzing in me as well. I spend the subsequent 24 hours in a functional panic attack, fear of seroconversion, pros and cons of the 30-day-after post-exposure-phophylaxis pill. If I take it will I be off work for weeks. If I take it will it eat my kidneys. But if I ask him about HIV he will feel differently. Fuck it. "P.s", I texted "have you bb-ed other guys since last getting tested?" He said no. I chose to trust the same man who broke it/mine. I figured, then, as now, that there are shades of honesty: coming in me is most definitely a dog move; but to lie about tests (and who he's slept with since) would be toxic, curse, foul play, bastardry. Evil.

*

"Been good but busy" he would say, but then, when we later met, he'd watched everything that had since come out on Netflix. Mmm hmm. Busy.

*

He thought it was clear. *We met, you know, on Grindr. And it was always my place.* Always his place. So, you're less of a fuckwit... if you're upfront about it? So, he didn't hear me when I asked, time and again, *why not my place? What do you have against it?*

*

"Sorry," he texted, 4 hours late. "Still with friends". Oh, no worries. See you at 2am, after cancelling my plans. "The lover's fatal identity is precisely: I am the one who waits" (Barthes).

*

He texts me to go to the Bowl for a gig (he likes me). I get a $50 Uber that gets lost on the way (it's worth it). He meets me at the gate (he likes me), he says hey, sorry, we should leave (he ... likes me?). He says it's shit inside. Don't want to waste your money (too late). There are no pass outs, anyway (he ... planned this?). Let's hang out in the park (he feels bad?). Let's take the tram back (he's not fucking serious?).

*

What does it mean? Why did he bring me? How to crack the case when there is only his word and my doublethink. Months pass. "I do genuinely like spending time with you" (liar? fuck up? who is it that is clueless?).

*

The same foncusion spreads to 'who-he-was': (1) he went out every w/e, he texted me drunk, he was a party boy with no substance but (2) he did an art-y project on kale, he scored a scholarship to study abroad, he once described a chat as an "airing of grievances". He's intelligent? Interesting? And (3) he stopped doing hard drugs, he tried Octsober and his display pic, when we cybermeet, is of him on a hike, in a cute lil wide rimmed hat = there is more to him? = he's DTE and not just down to fuck / to get fucked up? Did he not seem sort of innocent (if not naive)? He said, for one thing, that it was his first time on Grindr (or was that bullshit?). There was, as well, that time we had a joint and his bff *declared* it, as in "omg we're getting high", as if this too were a first, and they weren't as hardcore (i.e., too cool for me) as I'd believed. Nor did he seem like the scheming type—if only because he was the kind of dude who takes life at face value, goes with the flow, etc., *having not had a problem with it.*

*

He told me he just wanted to live his "best single life" (always with the on-trend turns of phrase, but a lil too often or out of context; proof not that—to paraphrase Avril Lavigne— he was acting like someone else, but that there was something more to him than the culture's cookie cutters [and so, for the lover, *allure*]).

*

Turn it off, he said once. The rain sounds so much better.

*

That he had an interior life ("I feel like wearing stripes") was a vista, a sprawl like the deep sea. To know his mind—to feel not skin but self, not lips or tips but the man as he was— live streamed from the brain stem, would be E, would be amphetamine. No waiting to get to know him. There he would be, laid bare of masks, guesses, shrouds, questions. For "isn't knowing someone precisely that - knowing his desire?" (Barthes).

*

I asked him where he sees himself x years down the line. What I really meant is what his life will look like without me (although, of course, I am looking at it already). The impulse is a bad one, thought-sadist that I am, and born as it is of a wish in the unconscious (actual question: could you ever see yourself with me?). The answer stings, a bit, but they are words for which my interpretant is split: travel, he says, and money, a job, go corporate. Okay. So. Is he (1) a boring status-anxious player scrambling to assemble the signs of "success" or (2) a humble, middle class hustler tryna keep up with the capitalocene? As if this could, somehow, be clarified (I am at a loss for which is true of me, let alone of him).

9.

Three dreams since:

1. I move in to his room when he leaves the country. Have we met already?

2. I meet his three brothers, who look more or less like him. (Aside: should I maybe ask an analyst why I like him more *because* of this?).

3. I go through our texts to copy the letter I sent him, but I accidentally 👍 the *post* and he gets a notification - *six months later*. He video calls me and chats as if it were water off his back. Also, he is at a party, having a great time, sipping on a cocktail in the sun. Meanwhile, I am languishing in frozen Hellbourne.

10.

Wondering if it is by seeing the love object as 'perfect' that any difference between us, however small, is a fault in me and objectively 'bad' e.g. how he always had the latest apps and lifehacks (I must be out of touch), how he said he kissed his straight guy friends in high-school (I must've been boring), how his ex moved from Denmark to be with him (I had no such ex → I must not be worth it), how he had lived abroad with him first (I'd only done sojourns → I must be sheltered). Add to this a kind of ressentiment. What if ... I could have been happy, only that I didn't go after it? What if I'd stopped the complex from ever taking root?

*

I set the perfect trap. The idea was, okay, life sucks, but this is just the set up. The scene is just right—age 18-21, you're stuck in a sleepy little burb, you work in a deadbeat job, you haven't met the right people. But you're young. And when you get out, you will be happy. You set a loose deadline—when you move, when you get your look right, when you master your craft and so on, your dream job/man/crew/life will drop in your lap, as planned. But then, quite suddenly, the time comes when you thought you'd be happy. Did you make the wrong moves? Or are you still incubating? And what of all these people who were already living that life when you were still making excuses? The glass breaks. You should have already been doing what you were really just looking forward to. How many guys have I met who were in love, who had boyfriends, at the age that I was waiting around for something to happen? How many who jumped ship at sixteen and found their tribe in the big city? Who followed their bliss—writing or DJing or whatever—and are, by now, lauded for doing it? How many who did not wait for the narrative arc to sweep them up but lived the life they wanted from the beginning?

*

I think, as well, of the skin flaws I thought would ruin me: the gash from the lamp that fell on my face, the pimpleosaur on my nose, the dry, red, flakey cheeks, the traitorous ingrown arse hairs. He said lol he wouldn't judge me for a pimple and I thought, then as now, of the razor bumps on his jaw; how they somehow made me like him all the more.

*

Meanwhile, I was in my first year out of uni—where writing, as a discipline, was on par with 'respected' 'professions' (+ where it did not matter if the writing was working out since I was still 'studying'). Now, having graduated, having lost the *get-out-questions-free* card, my life story turns ugly. I have 0.00 idea what I am doing and am, inwardly, a dropkick.

*

For years I was cool with how I looked on account of being *thin*. Body positive cause I hit the mini jackpot on the gene pool. I might have had a hook nose, a lil asymmetry, a hairy arse crack, a right ball smaller than the other, and so on, but at least I had the small bod that the top types would love, right? The slight of stature that would make them feel more man: more 20th century masc with a twiggy boy in the grip of their vice. Gym bunnies go forth and workout. Models count your calories, I had the auto-okay body to fall back on. What a slap in the ego, then, to hear that what he really wanted was to "sexually experiment" with someone *bigger than him. Someone taller.* Someone "perfect" for it. Someone, I submitted, who was just like him. Oh no, he said, flagging the gay stereotype of boys who go with boys that look just like them (see e.g. boyfriendtwins.tumblr.com [now defunct]). Oh no, I thought, guess I got it wrong: no opposites attracting, just mirrors in pools fringed with the petals of narcissus.

*

But there's good in him … isn't there? Like when he said "only if you're okay with it". Like when he said you're doing good when he first tried to fuck me. Like when he checked if I was okay when he was inside me. Like when he cat sat for a friend. Like when he asked me what I wanted for breakfast. Like when he texted me to tell me that he voted. Like when he told me to get home safe (every time). Like when he said he didn't want to be "that guy" (twice). Like when texted to say he was sorry. Like when he said he wished we'd talked sooner.

*

Try as I might to make him an archetype (the sleaze, the conniver, the player), I knew too much to sum him up as a villainy trope. Take e.g. the tics and fixed traits: what, in other words, could be no reflection (good or bad) of how he felt for me. Inexplicably endearing in the moment: how he had bad posture; how his fave food was pizza; how he was kind of a quiet guy; how he had a sort of monobrow; how he would shhh me during sex; how he'd grind his teeth in his sleep; how he'd shave his chest hair; how kissing in the street was "weird"; how he always came in missionary; how he was cool with staying in on a Saturday; how he abbreviated of course → 'ofc'; how his pocket sized room was always N&T; his unassuming style; his toothy grin; the gummy mouthguard he wore to bed; how these things disclosed a person, meaning not wholly good nor wholly bad, but merely—him.

11.

New Years, 2019. 'Shallow' by Gaga pops up in the playlist and I cry about how he wasn't there and would not want to kiss me—just as (when I asked him, at the tram stop, how he felt about PDA) he just sort of hugged me. *Hugging's nice*, he said. Hugging's nice.

*

'Shallow' being the original song for a movie I asked him out to see. Ha. We never did see a movie. Were we even dating?

*

Then, just as things were turning to things-past, he texts me for sex. I bite his head off; we meet but don't break up (since we were, as he made clear, never together). I pen a text but do not send it, for who could it be for? The ghost of him?

"You said you didn't know I was still so angry. I said I wasn't, but I lied. How could I not be angry when—after telling you that the sex, the late night texts and the booty calls were breaking my heart—you did it again. You said you thought that we were good after talking. Sorry? Did you not hear me, or did I go too easy? I laid my heart out and you still could not see it.

You said you didn't know how I felt. It was a shock, it seems, to hear that I cried for you. You said I hid how I felt. But I call bullshit. How could you have missed all the signs? How keen I was to see you? How I could not stop kissing you? How I fell into your eyes and could not look away?

You said to me that you "didn't think I was the type". The type for what? The type to care? The type to feel? To have passion? The type to be alive? If that's my type, then so be it. I would not have it any other way.

You said you didn't know me at all. But whose fault is that? You never made an effort. I thought I knew you, but I guess it goes both ways. I should've known from how you always bailed, how you always flaked, how I never seemed to see you by the light of day. I should have seen you for who you are."

TL;DR: Fuck you, man. You ate my heart.

12.

Me, chatting to my brother: "You think you've got a thick skin, you know? I mean, it's not the first time I've been rejected. I get rejected every day on the apps. I get rejected on dates. I get rejected by the guys who don't text me back. I get rejected at gigs where I go home alone. It's cool. But with him it was different. He saw me. He got to know me, man. And he wasn't into it. That hurts, you know? Because you are rejected not for how you look, but for who you are. It is your soul they turn down."

*

Although when I say 'they' I am of course still referring to him in the abstract "though this person may have shifted to the condition of a phantom" (Barthes).

*

Me, to myself: "I was meant 'to be ready for him'. That was the deal, see. No scouring the earth for a man prince. I'd live. I'd dress my best. Eat right. Write hard. Work out. Nice house. I'd be me and then we'd meet," a solar eclipse. But I got it all wrong. Sol rising yet not quite folding the moon, the stars having moved on me. Where. Where. Where. Where did I go wrong? And why can't time be bent? Chaos tamed?

13.

Autumn.

*

Rosehip oil, mist diffuser, no-stain deodorant, linen seared in the sun through his window. Still, I can't recall his scent. A warm, creamy, earthy what? Then, when he is long gone, I try truffle fries. Aftertaste *de toi*.

*

It stings that he left no photo trace, no ephemera for a memory box. It was a boon that, when stalking him on Insta, he had only one photo (and not a selfie). Proof that we were a match. Then—when he had already cut me off— he popped up on Tinder (back in the game), freezing my appdiction. Should I swipe left to the ether or right to match, when he might have swiped on me months ago? I wait it out. Days pass. Fina-fucking-ly the app refreshes, and his face disappears. I did not think to save the pics, but also, good riddance. His face is by then a bad sketch, a diffusing recall, and I, by some miracle, kept up the self-ban on looking him up (again). I want nothing more than to look—except, of course, to forget.

*

But just as his face was fading, I hear a voice as like his as any, on a podcasted episode of 3CR 'Queering the Air'. A soft-spoken drawl, a deep voiced Perth boy presenter. "Yeah, cool …" he says, at seemingly every opening, a sonic mirror of how *mon amour* would do the same. How hungry I'd been for his speech, for the utterances that could (*contra* to his body, his behaviour) tell me something true, when really what he said seemed to speak without saying much of anything ("yeah, it's chill"). Breadcrumbs, as ever. Also classic Melbourne fuckboi tip-toe-on-egg-shell strategy: speak and/or share enough to keep em cuming, but keep it vague, opaque, open to misreading, gaslighting, doublespeak, *chill.*

*

Thus, morsels of what he once said—mere sound bites of a man—play over and over in my inner-ear, as if they were the parting words of the now dead. "So many albums" he said once, of my Spotify screen. Were there? But of course he was a single guy, pun very much intended; listening, as he did, to an infinite list of playlists called e.g. 'bedroom chill'. Try as I might to recall his favourite genres, artists, styles, etc. (desperate to piece together his 'identity') there is only that long, long list of playlists. Or have I merely forgotten?

*

The body does not, however, emboss. Day and night I get to work with my metal tongue cleaner. They're big in Asia, he'd said, in his bathroom mirror, showing them to me. "They have ads for them on TV." I am thinking now if any of his microbes live on in my mouth, or if I cleaved them all out with the stainless steel band that he, himself, got me onto. Thinking as well if other bits of him (his germs, his DNA) colonised my innards, or if all that's left over is this twice daily routine; a dental hygiene, Dawkinian meme. Thinking, also, of how I still cling-wrap avocado halves the way I was shown by my ex in '09: first lay the plastic flat on the open face of the fruit, then pull it tight and twist the excess in a spindle at the back. A taut mask that keeps the avo fresh. A kitchen trick, a mere muscle memory of a boy I used to kiss.

14.

Oh, Molly Burch he said, when he saw her on my Spotify. As if she were a friend and he were holding counsel, giving advice: oh Mol, how are you still not over him? How are you still lamenting him in song? I did not know then that I would soon have Burch on an infinite loop, a waxy balm for my scars. Oh Jack, he would say, when I told him that he had not left me in such a good place; that I'd spilled tears. Don't be sad, he said then, don't be sad oh Jack, oh Burch, oh the downhearted. Stranger to heartbreak? Or skeptic of the reasons? "Historical reversal: it is no longer the sexual which is indecent, it is the sentimental—censured in the name of what is in fact only another morality" (Barthes). Why should it be like a breakup, he said, when there was nothing between us. When it was clearly nothing.

*

I find, in Burch's albums—*Downhearted* and, later, *First Flower*—an emotional volta, as if each of them were one long sonnet. The first turns at the mid-way point (track: 'Fool'); and the other at track #9 ('True Love'). It's a change not in subject matter but in general sentiment, diving from melancholy and present-tense limerence to something more like dissolute pain; to despair. These post-turn tracks are soon my faves, there where I know my own catharsis lay waiting. Time being time, I put them on to rip the wounds that I want, now, to commit to words. I look for a volta in 'what happened' to me also: side A bearing the sadness of longing, of yearning, while Side B, ex post heartbreak, is me staring into space, stilted, in shock at how much more it hurt than I'd ever imagined.

*

The selfsame tracks that get me weeping: that "truest of messages", writes Barthes, meaning "those of my body, not that of my speech". For words, he says—quoting Schubert—"what are they? One tear will say more than all of them." That, or a good tune.

*

To say nothing of what I played when things were good (viz., when I was deluded into thinking he was mine). *Berhana*, self-titled. *Nikes*, Frank Ocean. Both, somehow, a part of this piece (insofar as they add to it something words alone could not). But surely not mere... atmosphere? *Again with the ineffable.*

*

I am still apt, at times, to think of him as a heartless fuck, a callous attack, manvoid of feelings. But a light goes on and I think of how he, too, had known of Burch. Recognised her. So. Had he, too, been algorithmically matched to love songs? Holes in the souls? Had he, too, been broken hearted? Flash point. Quicksand. I find myself hoping that he *had*, that he was now, and that he would be in pain again; no loving kindness left, my self warps, twists, distorts. I want for him not just a just-deserts, but a hurt that is ensnared in the memory of me, me, me. How does it feel, mate? How does it taste? Think of me when you say of others: you broke my heart, you seared my soul, I'm hurting.

*

Yeezus, what bitter ends.

*

I mean obviously he does 'think of me', if only because I am the subject of a memory, just as I think of guys for whom I had ambiguous feelings (but which is no less a remembrance of things past). But they can too soon turn to toxin; a favourite game of former lovers. *What if I was wrong about them? Should I maybe text them?* And if I am having these thoughts about others would He, too, think of texting me? Danger zone, baby.

*

It was Burch who tipped me off that I had, after all, been in love; when, that is, I went from liking her songs to identifying 'with' them. Gone now is the shame I apportioned to folk who think pop/alt songs are "about them". No, no, none of that—now I feel relief, tension diffusing ("your music saved me", people say of idols and divas, @-ing them on social media, and this, finally, makes sense to me). I think of quoting the Burch verses that could just as well have been the voice-over in an art-film version of my blackened heart. I wait for the volta, play the sad tracks and jot down the phrases that rattle my ventricles. But it is soon obvious that I am copying out the songs in full, an art-event that would be better and more lawfully executed by a public Spotify playlist. I think, too, of how he will never read these words for which the best-destiny is a low-run, DIY chapbook of maybe 20 copies, a booklet I would peddle at a zine fair he will never attend—never read, or never really hear—as compared with lyrics of a song that I could play at gig in the city (would it that I were more like Burch) or upload to the network, where the Great Algorithms might one day catch up with him ... again? All of which is to say: I am still ideating 'the getting back in with him'.

*

In becomes, in retrospect, a romance in three parts: the rapture of meeting, the ecstasy of hanging out (such as it is) and, of course, the anxiety that it will all be lost. But, as Barthes notes, there is of course no such chronology. It was always already all three.

15.

On the tram, on the cusp of crying again: "What am I doing wrong here? There is nothing wrong with me. I'm a nice guy. I'm not ugly. I'm interesting. I'm funny. I'm a good root. I should be a catch. I'm doing everything right but nothing's fucking happening for me. Why? Why? Why?"

*

In the aftermath I pare back my wardrobe, finding everything too flashy; shave my head, shoutout to Britney; up my training to get 'ripped', spurred on not by these changes in themselves but in the Spartan absence of feeling for them. To be less like who he once met, perhaps (or more like his "equal") but above all to feed the will not to care; to lay down worldly feels altogether. "To be ascetic," writes Barthes. "I shall (hysterically) signify my mourning (the mourning which I assign myself) in my dress, my haircut, the regularity of my habits."

*

New year, new me, no you. I go on into dating hyperdrive, fucking some of them, feeling none of it. It is not so much rebound as mind-elsewhere. At first I count them up like digits in

my net worth, as if to prove that life goes on—
and bursts—in spite of him. I think of keeping
a list, giving each guy epithets and sobriquets,
but quickly lose count / forget. Still: I hold them
up against the thin, microslide memory of the
(alleged) One, each of them falling short for no
reason except that they are not him.

*

On the street, I seem to see him in double-
exposure: thick brows, thick hair, stubble,
chinny grin, etc. The more they are like him,
the more I seem to like them. Who is my type,
he asked at the very end; and I very nearly said,
simply, You. Much as I may resent the fact, the
bottom-line, socially effected truth is that I fell
for how he looks and/or presents. Sure, it helped
that he kept me on my toes (Wilde: "The very
essence of romance is uncertainty") but it was
his beauty that—unlike his behaviour—had
an absolute clarity; *radiant*, as Plato put it, or
"appearance itself" to borrow from Gadamar;

in short a beauty that flies from words but that was so bright as to be self-evident, free from any hermeneutics. It was, in a word, divine. As was he, by proxy.

*

That, and the more elusive *he (might) love me back*.

*

In a rant to a mate: "I feel cheated: not by him, but by the world. I never, ever like anyone this much ... and have them maybe like me back. Never. It just doesn't happen. Then, I meet this guy, and feel it *all*. Feel everything. And for what? It was nothing. He felt nothing. Look, I know the gods aren't out to get me. I get it. But I have only my life to go by here, and it's not looking good. It's been, I don't know, ten years. Is this really how much I'll hit it off with guys? Once in a decade?" Or once in an epoch, when the dust from this life is a strata of rock? What a cruel rock it is, this earthy grave to-be.

16.

Meanwhile everyone I've ever met has always already been in mutual love since their balls dropped—two, three, an infinity of happy fucking couples since they turned sexteen. I mean when the fuck did you live? Where did you find the years? What makes you so goddamned special? I grow to loathe them, as if they only left the house to strut their love in my face. *Je deteste* every pair I see in the streets, seemingly effortless bonds upon which I cast dark thoughts. I hope he snores. I hope he cheats on you. I hope your sex dries up. I hope in the end you are ripped apart and you never love again.

*

An anxiety swells to the effect that I have no 'community' and that I'm losing what is, in the end, a numbers gayme. He, for one, had none of the tumult of not-meeting-guys. And was that why? He had the gay friends, he liked the gay bars, and so on, while I was whiling away the weekends on goon-y *soirées* with a mostly hetero group of mates, sealed off from the 'scene'.

*

When I asked him, for the 69th time, if not-douching was a problem, he referred to advice he'd heard on gay podcasts which I'd later look up and gorge upon. But I'd stay mostly gay-less in my circle, defaulting to the-gays-are-for-dating pattern. Look, I'm not avoiding them IRL, but I have friends already. Straight, yes, but that's no reason to drop em. They're the best friends I've ever had. And who the fuck makes kin for the sake of better odds?

*

I want to talk about first love not as a hippocampal scar, but as a philosophical problem: sold, as I was, on the binary of the closet vs a 'normal' life, in which love "just happens" ... as it does in bow-tied romcoms and proverbs ft. fish in the sea, or love when you "least expect it". You can see where this is going. What better stuff for confirmation bias than a surety of love. Let no wisdom speak of being inevitably lonely. Let the tragedies die with the bard. For "what sense of hope or satisfaction could derive from an ending like that?" (Briony, *Atonement*, 2007). But the *a posteriori* of experience rubs up against what I am sick to fucking death of in the discourse: it happens, it happens, it just happens. Cool, thanks for the platitudes, please fuck off with your common non-sense.

*

Let's look at the odds, which are about as good as getting to Uranus. First up kill off the straight ppl (1/10,000). Next, wait to meet a guy in the street or at work (1/1,000,000), i.e., say goodbye to serendipity. Oh well. Try matchin on the apps (1/100). Now see who even answers (1/10). Ask if they want to hang out before you both die (1/99999999). Nice. Do they want to meet up again (1/69)? Great. Now check if you can still stand them (approx 1/1000). Guess you got lucky. Do they want to maybe date for a bit more (~1)? Cool. Now run the numbers on both sides (= 0). Oops. Better luck in your next life.

*

Just a heads up that this piece—like the subject matter—is also going nowhere. The ends stay loose. The plot doesn't twist. There is, strictly speaking, no story arc; a writerly 'trick' that, I know I know, sounds about as pretentious as building a "community" of "craft beer" "connoisseurs". But that's how things panned out with *him* ... which is to say they didn't. Things don't seem to pan out, period. It's a fucking mess. And that is precisely what's at stake for me.

*

"Perhaps you're not really putting yourself out there," a guru tells Charlotte, on S05EP02 of *Sex and the City.* "No, she's out there" answers Carrie. "Believe me, she's there." But am I? Listen, I thought I was a pretty balanced guy —

a lil work, a lil play, drinks from time to time. But I keep meeting extra-extra-extroverts who literally get up at 8, go to the gym, go to yoga, go to a class, go to work, go for lunch, go for dinner, go for drinks, catch up, go on a date, go for drinks again, meet a friend, make a friend, get home at I don't know 3am and do it again and again, every farken day. And I'm just like, cool, so am I a hermit? Isn't a date a week, on average, pretty good? Drinks on Friyay? I mean isn't that enough?

*

Then—just as my sense of self is imploding—a guy I'm dating gets me onto Myers-Briggs. I do the test. Yeah, he says, thought you'd be INFJ. Okay. I still have NO idea if that's good, or how one should live. Yeah I know, be true 2 u, blah blah blah. But what if being 'you' means you're kind of fucked? Objectively speaking? As my friend text-raged: "why is it SO hard to just have a good time and connect???".

*

"You have a good body" says some dude I'm dating.

The next day, he ghosts me.

It's all good but what the fuck? Are people doing math when they think of me? Good body (yay). Not so funny (nay). And that's just the credit-debit, double book-keeping weighing up of me. Too bad if it's a straight up deal-breaker. I'm thinking e.g. of when I hit on some guy at a party but a friend has done the legwork already, and proceeds to let me down gently. He is, she frowns, only into guys with beards. Ummm. Okay. Cool. So, no flexibility? Just the beards? Cue the familiar dribble about a guy who MUST be taller than you. Taller? Really? Literally just higher than you, vertically? That's your necessary and sufficient condition?

*

Suddenly there's an angel on my left shoulder, too, saying *Yes, Jack but you got scouted by an agent at Sydney Airport in 2014 and have been told by 1 in 25 people that you "should be a model" while* the devil on the right says *True but you have been single for a decade and, to quote the guy you will date 12 months after finishing this piece, "if it were purely mental it would be perfect" (soooo not so hot after all).* How about this: don't fucking tell me I'm pretty if I'm not.

*

Look, it's not as if I'm not getting hits. There are also guys who have been into me, but didn't get the feels back. And since I like about 1 guy per two years there are, in fact, fewer of those guys than the ones into me. But it's beside the point, blunted though it is. What is inexplicable is the *not clicking.*

*

Could it really be another trick of statistics? That for some people I really am weird or boring or hot but for as many others I'm not? That at the end of the day I have just met a > number of people than could all meaningfully agree on what I am like? Ergo hotornot.com, where I could tally this up and *get an average.*

*

In a note to self: "Is it just me or are ppl getting hotter as my love luck gets shitter?". I thought it was a trick of the socials but what if this is, in fact, just the real world—in which I'm fugly / a fuck up, relative to other people. Not a conscientious objector to "trying hard" but just honest-to-god shitter. It does not help, of course, to have made a life in the inner-inner-inner city, the original, living, breathing 'feed' where there is inevitably someone looking and/or doing 'better'.

*

The gay-disney-story goes: you come out, you flock to gay meccas and you get to make up for lost time. The worst is behind you; the best is at your backside. It "gets better"—right? But the facts are against me. Sure, it's safer. But I don't know that it's much nicer. Look, I don't want to gay bash. It's not a Judas/Brutus kiss. But the scene, for me, is no utopia. It's tough out there, folks. You gotta be seen. You gotta walk the walk. You gotta talk the talk. You gotta look the part. You gotta know the right 'people'. The scene/seen is cliquey as fuck. And that's just the stuff you can work, if you want it. Fingers crossed you're a white, anglohandsome endomorph as well. And you better hope to fuck you got tucked into insta (or 'the gram' as the youth would say) by your first year of high school (cause that's who you are now). Is he hot or not? Cool and/or 'connected'? / Hey, I'm friendly. I'm pretty fucking easy going. But I'm tired of being judged at the gaytes of hell. I don't know if my brain can stand to 'meet' any 'new' 'people' who think I'm a joke, who lift their brows, who post my pics in group chats as an e.g. of what not to be, or who literally just get up and walk off in the bar, not having adequately proved myself. Sorry boys, I have my mental health to think about.

*

Yeah, it's just my experience. But also sorry-not-sorry if I'm an empiricist.

*

Peak hurt: his best single life had, he said, been no such thing. It has so far felt "empty". Empty. I took this personally, a slight of hand like a shiv to my liver. Thanks, man. Nice to know that I have filled you with nothing but my spit; that I have helped to dig an abyss, making space in your spirit while filling none of it.

*

I have never in my life both loved and resented someone (one wants to say hate, of course, but only in the throngs of being love sick) in more or less equal measure, wishing them both perfect rapture and a pain to match my own.

I ♥ed him.

I (ʻ—ʻ)ed him.

I want him in my marrow forever, and also somewhere off-world where I would never ever have to see him.

*

But why? For not 'giving me a chance'? The (+) wish has within it a negativising poison. It is *pharmakon*: please will you try, expend, put in effort. Yet why should I want someone to have to try to want to like me? "Don't let guys treat you like free salsa. You are extra guacamole, baby" (some guy on Grindr).

*

Some solace in the fact that how I felt for him has by now *spilled*. Other men stand out as they never had, as if he had been my first and it was, in the end, just another awakening.

17.

But my type is unchanged. In a text to a friend: "Yeeeaahhh [that question] is my life - why I like straight/masc presenting guys, and why they don't like me, and on and on. My brain's split two ways: [is it] internalised homohating which is no less a kind of prejudice that can be overcum OR a sexual perversion that is no different from liking feet or having your balls nailed to a board [which], like those predi lick tions, is just who you are and what you're into. It's … not so much my opinion as my dilemma. I just don't know the answer."

*

To borrow from Luke of the 'Gays are Revolting': *We want to fuck what oppressed us. The guys who hurt us worst.* Why else this soft spot for basic white guys who don't have lisps, the high school sweethearts I skipped back then?

*

He was, after all, straight passing; 'normal'; 'ordinary'; so not-rainbow-gay as to make me ask, after years of feeling at home with being unusual, doubtful of the norm, skeptic of the common, and so on, if I could have found peace in dressing like a 'regular' guy, speaking like a regular' guy, watching breakfast news, liking more less the same thing as the average person, following more or less mainstream trends, and so on.

*

To be fair, I fell for an ideality that was all mine; propped him up as the straight-acting homme of my Freudian, teen-brain; the heteronormative big spoon that would desire me as the Other. Meanwhile he himself was on the lookout for a man of his own making: an equal, with the "perfect dick"—"not too big, not too small" (ouch?)—who would presumably be to him what, in a way, he was to me.

*

Feeling hoodwinked, but what gives me the right? Who was I to pigeonhole him in the dream of 'us'? And who the fuck is this, anyway, falling foul of straight gender roles?

18.

From the text I never sent: "I told you that since what happened (or didn't), I have been unsure of everything: who I am, what I want, how people see me. You said I should not change who I am for you, or anyone else. But you missed the point. It's not change but a loss of faith ... in myself. That shakes a person. That fucks with them."

*

How can one be sure of anything when they were wrong about what they were surest of? In a Fb message to a friend, Jan 12, 2019: "(Psycho) logically, I get it: he was just not that into me. But, spiritually, I am at a loss. How could it be, in effect, a ruse? A false alarm? A fool's gold?" What happens is that the doubt spreads, malignant. It starts with, "how was I wrong about us". But it grows across the cortex. I thought I was OK looking but what if, gasp, I'm biased? I thought I was pretty awesome but what if I'm boring as fuck? I thought I was pretty good at writing, too, but then so does every other wannabe.

*

Take a problem for which there is no answer in the literature, in reputable sources or the wisdom of sayings. Take a problem like 'how did he feel'. I could not read his mind, and he would not come clean. Take a problem like how to spend your time: stick to writing, or try a litany of new things in case you missed your true calling? How can you be sure that you have skipped a beat, missed a ship, let *eudaimonia* elude you? No good saying "trust your gut" or "you just know", since it is precisely those presumptions that are at issue. I'm a skeptic and a fallibilist and at a loss for what is best. I'm not sure. I don't know. I thought for sure that you were for me also.

*

There being nothing to lean on. "Isn't it rather," asks Barthes, "that I remain suspended on this [one] question, whose answer I tirelessly seek in the other's face: *What am I worth?*". The locus of my undoing: my two go-to measures of self (do guys like me / is my work good) had, in him, a synergy that was emptier than either one of them. A symbiosis that goes: My work is no good, so I have nothing to show for myself, so why would he like me OR I've wasted my time on this, so I have no life, so I have no money, so I have no status, so why would he like me OR I'm a cultural cliché, an art fraud, an imposter, a ghost of the gentrified, so why the fuck would he like me. And on and on it goes, burning up my circuits.

*

Because what is the mental test for when you know you're good at writing? So far I've taken cover under "it feels right" to "it sounds good", but what if, objectively, the test is something completely fucking different? What if it is a technicality that, because I do not have nearly as good a mastery as I think, I am completely unaware. Take my 'voice' for instance. I've long since shed Standard English prose, finding the prosody far too stiff and starchy, the lexis like a straight jacket, the sentence deaf to the sentence on the internet, the sound apparently unaware that rap ever happened. I like my sentences phat with maximalism, full to the brim with allusions and delusions and the sounds with which I'd inflect my words in person (for better or worse). It's all in the name of expression at the expense, perhaps, of decorum. Let's not forget that I mostly write txts (who doesn't?) and also I learned to open up over a bottle of red and a street drug. Why should these *paroles* be tamed? That's my 'voice'. That's who I 'am'. That's what I'm good at ... isn't it? Alright, yeah, my words could be nothing more than a lens-distortion of Nietzsche-at-the-end, the ramblings (with the syntax to match) of someone completely out of touch with what is actually good or in good taste. It wouldn't surprise me. I've been wrong before (clearly). But what's the alternative? Shall I start my craft from scratch and try to please the other 20% of people?

*

I test the waters and enter an earlier incarnation of this piece to some prizes. When it comes in second for a prize in Arizona the friendly editors offer to share their feedback. This, to me, is nothing short of a small miracle; a splendid fairy wren in a desert. As I once put it, in an email to a journal, "of the 150+ submissions I made [this year], this is—without exaggeration—the only entry for which I received a meaningful response to my work". Having finally scored some *back of feed*, as my best friend would say, I read their email 20 times and soak it up like tea in a pot. I agree with much of what they say and start to draft the changes in my head. Great. Good. This is what I should do... right? Yeah? Who else watched that kid's claymation series *The Trap Door* in the 90s? I suddenly feel like Burke in the castle by the trap door, where "there is always something down there, in the dark, waiting to come out", only that in my case it is not a giant arachnid so much as the many species of doubt. What if, for instance, I have other people read the piece—people whose opinions I respect *at least as much*—and I get the opposite feedback? How should I feel about the editor's suggestions? How can I reconcile them? Know that I am not saying I should throw the feedback out. Like I said, I agreed with much of it. But that is a very different thing to knowing that they got it 'right'.

*

A new question: do I still have feelings for him, or are they effected by the text? Will they go away when it's finished, or am I making it worse, fossilising a crush that would otherwise have wilted? And—is it worth it?

*

This, then, is the catch of writing through pain in time. He is gone; it is over; I am feeling better. Meanwhile I insist on writing 'about it': not to relive the *amour*, but so as not to deny— as he did—its significance. Something loosely sacrificial: an offering of triggers and dips in mental health "for" the art object in which how I felt is—in its own, small way—given space (credence?). This is memory as a vineyard: ripe for harvest, with grapes for vino and the bowels of cellar doors; for new forms of meaning. All the same: how to one-up time at the risk of pain-in-presence when the pay off is, at best, a paraphrase of reality in a language that makes little difference to it.

*

The love object, as Barthes laments, is by its very nature not listening. Words won't make him love you. They won't hurt him to read, or to hear. They won't impress him, glitter though they may. Too late for that. If anything, it would be a pain to sit through and — much like being lovelorn IRL—embarrassingly one-sided. *C'est tout.*

*

Soz Foucault (via Miller, by way of Wikipedia) who notes that, since first doing homework for a cute guy in school, he has—all along—been "trying to do intellectual things that would attract beautiful boys". As far as I can tell doing intellectual things is about as good for getting guys as freshly trimmed toe hair. It doesn't hurt, but thaz about it.

*

And then the editing? And then the re-writing? And then the re-reading when, give or take a few Gibbous moons, it is all over? I mean even the writing that predates him has stalled to the point that work from years ago—work that I do not even think my best—is still pending on Submittable, while the new / 'mature' words are queued up in folders on my Mac … a long, long way from peer validation. I think of how to get around this. I think of retro-dating old work so that it is tied not to the date of appearance but to the blocks of my life in which it was written: 2015-17, 2017-19, 2019-20, etc. But for what? Vindication?

*

Thought runs with ways to make him regret it. I'll look my best. I'll ignore you. I'll have left the country. He'll get in touch and I'll text back: "You had your chance and you blew it." Then he'll get whiteguy old, turning crinkle-cut in the skin, his "equal" looking no less worse for wear. Also he'll die alone. Naturally, none of these images help me along. On the contrary, I wriggle in the guilt, unsure of who in me is so blardy awful. Whose thoughts are these? Whose words of fury? But what then is this very piece, if not a will to revenge, an archiving of my version of him? Who, it asks, will desire him as I have? *Who will write about you again?*

*

In France, a friend digs up letters of obsession from her ex. She sends me a pic of an A4 leaf titled—in words he wrote in blood—"I Love You", filled from top to bottom, left to right with a maddened mantra, repeated over and over as if in the ditches of a dusty old record: ich Liebe dich, ich Liebe dich, ich Liebe dich, ich Liebe dich, ich Liebe dich. I make the necessary dich/dick joke and agree with her that the letter is übercreepy. But it dawns on me that I have been writing more or less the same thing, at first in my brain and now in these fugues (& for someone with whom I was something still less than an ex; to whom I can only refer, precisely, as a 'former lover'). No utterance seeming to capture their feelings, the writer turns words to rhythms, baser meanings like the drum of a heart or a techno beat. The same sound of a re-re-recollection of 'what happened'.

*

Who was it that said it did not, in the end, matter what I said in the texts to him? The point was that I texted, that I kept in touch. For months I parroted this idea to friends, as if saying made it so. I liked the idea but I never quite got through to myself. I texted as little as possible:

evasive action, fear of fucking up. Later, he said that past crushes would text him, like, five times a day. That was how he knew they liked him. Haha, I criedinside. Awesome.

*

What follows is a tumult of words as much as of dates. Never to be told again that I'd "hid" how I felt, I set out to be nek level direct and also literal in how I speak to guys. "This has been fun," I smiled to some Scottish lad, "Do you want to come to my house and have sex?". And then, to a videographer I dated but who would ultimately ghost me: "I really like you. I'd like to see more of you and also have sex with you". Sorry, but you have to spell it out for them. This becomes known to my friends as the 'Jack way', which is also how I ultimately 'get over it'. In other words, bye to the 'game' and hello to a way of speaking that cannot be accused of ambiguity. Also, I start texting guys 3-300 times a day. Hello. Hi. Did you get the fucking message?

*

A retrospective takes root saying, in effect: I would not have written anything, if only I had said everything to him aloud. 7ish years of taking writing 'seriously' but I was, it seemed, no better at communicating with the people who were actually in my life. Here language is to blame, and with it the preoccupation with 'writing about it'. If only I had got the message right at the time, I would not have had to write it after the fact. If only I brought— to the moment— the same faith, practice, focus, etc. that I bring, alone, to the dated word—well, who knows? My speech might, in other words, have serenaded him. Here writing is implicated as too little / too late; were my language only good enough 'in the first place'. I am reminded of how I grind my teeth when I read—as if the word as script were always only the word in retrograde, and it were trying, now, to get back 'out', via my boney mouth and onwards to an interlocutor.

*

But the "ego discourses only when it is hurt" (Barthes).

*

I am not even sure, myself, if there was in the end anything worth making this big a deal of, or if it was objectively a complete fucking joke. How are you supposed to know? As with day to day life, my litmus test has been how much it's been like video content. The story, such as it is, should be worthy of a scene in a movie or series, where the feelings are strongest, the speech is snappy, the action moves, the stakes are high and also the lighting is nice. But, this being bullshit, I have no choice but to fall back on words and the worlds that are born by them.

19.

Winter. I think of how the earth has moved, now, to where it was when we started. I think of the first thing I wrote but did not send to him.

*

NOT A LOVE POEM

420 anal in muted
linen, listening to your
indie / pop / Spotify
shuffle
and reading that the
feeling is mutual. yeah
i'll give everything a go
once or twice
in a night
except, of course,
making love
poems

i've tried jotting down
the pertinent
stuff, butt
they end up like
scribbly gum

lube smear lines;
a mess
in the recently
deleted cum detritus
bin, full of scrunched
up tissue paper with
boystuff wasted
on it.

sure i wanna wring
the men from the
towels and make them
mine, were it not for flings
and the waste of finger
tips, taps and breath:
the past as a head of
broccoli,
the past as a big D:
i'll burn more
from the chew than
i'll get from swallowing.

***

not a love poem cause
"you had to be there".
but I was there and I am
still scared of the stroke
of a clock / cock cry for a
new day - just another dream.
okay, so, not a love poem but -
perhaps just a poem about

you.
about how you wanted
to start with a drink and
"go from there", about
how you put the rubber in
a tissue, cadeau, about how I fit
you like a glove and
you texted back tomorrow.

okay, so, not a love poem but
something about being chill
with the weed with the drink
about how you are the bee but
i tasted your anthers also,
about those sweet pits that
you put down to Rexona, about
the snuggling after.

riding your matte black bike
to the park to hang out (no catch)
"just to say hi" (for real),
kissing me from the side, and
the Spiderman kiss we tried,
napping on your bed
in the sun

how you asked if I was hungry
and if I want to keep hanging out after
eating (I did, I did, I did) and how we
found the same show funny and

how you may have just passed out and
how we made loose plans to re-hang out and
how you pushed me out your front door, gently

***

but not a love poem cause -
what if I get the spell
wrong, what if the charm
wears off or what if I
jinx it? touch wood, lol
why don't I stick to thinking
about you?

not a love poem cause what
happens when it's just a poem
viz, when it's just the frame or
the glass pane? will I smash you
on the ground? will I hit
delete(terious) boy? but no
worries, cause it's not a love poem

but a poem about you
being (mostly) vego about
loving how I "just wear trackies" about
your snow globe eyes about
how you "feel like a tea" about
the slip-off black shorts about
how you are chill and "yoghurt

is chill" and not a love
poem but one to remember,
not a love poem but one about
how you were the first time
I just had to try
a love poem
on.

2018-19

Contributors

EMMA ASHMERE's short story collection *Dreams They Forgot* (Wakefield Press 2020) follows her novel *The Floating Garden* (shortlisted Small Press Network Book of the Year 2016). Other publications include *Meanjin, Age, Overland, adda, Griffith Review.*

JACK BASTOCK is queer and does not eat animals. He is a graduate of the creative writing program at the University of Melbourne, with recent work appearing in *LandLocked Magazine, The Decadent Review* and *Hotel Amerika.* Jack lives in Melbourne/Naarm with friends, and on the internet with you.

JENNY BLACKFORD writes poems and stories for people of all ages, often with a tinge of magic, science, or deep time. And cats. Her work has been published in journals and anthologies including *Going Down Swinging*, *Westerly*, *Strange Horizons* and *Cosmos*.

BROOKE FORBES is a first year law student at University of Newcastle, also holding a Bachelor of Communications and Masters in Business Administration. She has 10 years of media and tech business development experience.

QUINN EADES is a researcher, writer, poet, and gutter philosopher. He is the author of *all the beginnings: a queer autobiography of the body*, and *Rallying*, and is currently working on a book-length collection of fragments written from the transitioning body, titled *is the body home*.

EMILY JAMES is a film production and creative writing student at UTS who loves storytelling above all things (unless there's chocolate around.) She has previously worked with *SpineOut* and *Good Reading* magazines as a reviewer.

PHOEBE LUPTON is a writer of mixed European and South Asian heritage, currently living on unceded Ngunnawal and Ngambri land. Her recent work has been published in *F*EMS Zine*, *Voiceworks* and *Kill Your Darlings*.

BROOKE MADDISON is a writer working on Turrbal and Yuggera land. Her work has been published in *Antithesis*, *Colloquy*, *Kill Your Darlings* and *Verity La* and she is currently working on her debut novel.

CHRISTOPHER MARCATILI is a queer fiction and non-fiction writer. He's published short works in print and online and has been putting the finishing touches on a novel for too many years now. More at christophermarcatili.com

ANTHONY MARKEL is 19 years old and currently studying Year 12 VCE. He has a passion for literature and writing short stories and poetry. He identifies as a gay male.

ISABELLE QUILTY (they/them) is a young author from Newcastle, New South Wales, raised on a mix of Fleetwood Mac and Bollywood classics. They embrace their heritage by cooking traditional Fijian-Indian food and correcting people when they say 'chai tea.' 'My Strawberry Tea' was first published in the 2021 University of Newcastle Writing Club Anthology.

ERIN RILEY is a trans social worker who lives in Sydney on Gadigal Land. Erin's work has recently featured in *Kill Your Darlings* and in 2021, they received a Penguin Random House Write It Fellowship to develop their creative non fiction manuscript, *Wrestling With Feelings*.

LYDIA TRETHEWEY is a visual artist and author living and working in Perth, Western Australia. She teaches visual art at Curtin University.

TANYA VAVILOVA is a Russian-Australian writer preoccupied with liminal spaces and outsider perspectives—by life on the margins. Her debut collection of essays, *We are Speaking in Code*, was released in 2020.

ALLI SEBASTIAN WOLF (they/them/she/
her) is an award-winning multidisciplinary
artist based in Eora / Sydney, Australia.
They work across visual arts, performance,
costume, drag, playwriting, film and theatre.
Queer and gender fluid, their work explores
environmental, gender, and social themes with
a subversive playfulness.

Editors

BRONWYN MEHAN (she/her) is the founder of Spineless Wonders. She has worked as a high school English teacher, a creative writing teacher and freelance editor. Her writing has been published in *Best Australian Poetry*, *Meanjin*, *The Age* and *Sleepers Almanac*.

YGRAINE HELOISE (she/her) is a young writer, editor and illustrator living in New South Wales on Gundungurra land. She is currently studying a Bachelor of Creative Arts, majoring in Creative Writing, and in her spare time likes to read, write poetry in the notes app on her phone, and talk to her many plants. She is also writing and illustrating her own short poetry zine.

Spineless Wonders publications are available in print and digital format from participating bookshops and online. For further information about where to purchase our print and ebooks, go to the Spineless Wonders website:

www.shortaustralianstories.com.au